TAMING WES

BILLINGSLEY SERIES

MELISSA ELLEN

HONEY BEE PUBLISHING, LLC

Honey Bee Publishing, LLC

First Edition: November 2018
Printed in the United States of America

PROLOGUE
WES

Nine Years Earlier...

I punched through the side exit door, praying I didn't set off a silent alarm.

I needed air.

I *needed* to get my shit under control.

I turned the corner, leaning against the side of the old church that had been constructed in the middle of downtown Austin. I tilted my head back against the rough brick and closed my eyes, taking a deep inhale.

Reaching into my coat pocket, I pulled out the flask I had tucked inside. I twisted off the cap and wasted no time pouring the whiskey down my throat, hoping the burn as it slid would take the edge off, giving me something else to focus on other than this damn wedding.

"I hope you saved some of that for me."

With a slow turn of my head I looked over at the gorgeous bride-to-be as she sauntered toward me with a teasing smile on her face. She reached her hand out for the flask. I passed it to her without hesitation, watching her closely as she pressed her perfect lips against the bottle.

She squeezed her eyes shut, her face pinching as the bite of the liquor hit her throat. Fighting back a cough, she covered her mouth with the back of her hand, trying to pretend like the whiskey wasn't tough to swallow.

I grinned at her then glanced at our surroundings, wondering what the hell she was doing out here where anybody could see her. Granted, we were on the backside of the church and the likelihood was slim, it was still risky.

Unexpected.

An answered prayer.

"What are you doing out here? Isn't it bad luck or something to see the bride before the wedding?"

She rolled her eyes with a smile. "That only applies to the groom," she said, before taking one more shot straight out of the flask and passing it back to me.

I took it, taking one more of my own, before twisting the lid back on and tucking it away in my suit jacket. "Still doesn't explain what you're doing out here. *Alone.*"

"I'm not alone. I'm here with you," she countered, claiming the space beside me on the wall as she stared straight ahead, her mind seeming to drift.

It didn't surprise me at all she had little concern about messing up her dress. She'd always been laid back, since the day we met as kids. It's one of the many reasons why we clicked.

I shook my head at her avoidance, a slow smile taking over my face. I already knew the answer, even if she refused to say it out loud. She was hiding. From what, I wasn't sure.

After admiring how beautiful she looked for a few seconds, I playfully nudged my shoulder against hers to get her full attention. She looked over at me, our eyes connecting, a familiar crackle sparking between us as I held her gaze. It was that same spark I'd felt since I was seventeen. The one I refused to acknowledge.

"Talk to me, sweetheart. What's on your mind?"

A light sigh left her lips as she looked away from me again. There were a few beats of silence before she finally spoke. "It's nothing, really. Probably just the notorious cold feet everyone talks about."

I shoved my hands into my pants pockets, resisting the urge to reach for the flask again. The anxious energy that had lifted only moments ago returned. There was no sense in getting my hopes up.

"It's just...it's silly really..." She heaved another sigh, then straightened her small frame as she stepped away from the wall and turned to face me. "Dad said something jokingly and I'm overthinking it."

"You, overthink something? Never," I teased.

She laughed with a slight shake of her head as she looked down at her feet. "I know. Right?" She used her sarcasm to conceal her nerves.

"What did he say?"

She shrugged, her eyes looking everywhere but at me, her teeth gnawing on her bottom lip.

"Cricket?" I prodded some more with my old nickname for her. She was a tiny thing. Always had been. She was my little Jiminy Cricket, keeping me out of trouble my whole life.

She looked up, her eyes searching, her face full of apprehension. "He was only teasing me about how he'd been dreading this day since I was born...that for a long time he thought he'd be giving me away to *you* one day... Crazy, right?"

My heart raced with her words, with the way she looked at me expectantly. There was a hint of hopefulness in her eyes, or maybe I was just imagining it. I swallowed the knot in my throat as I tried to talk myself out of telling her how I really felt about her.

I'd been fighting my feelings for her since the night I almost kissed her on the tailgate of my truck. We were young then, barely figuring out the world for ourselves.

We'd been friends forever and I hadn't wanted to ruin what we had. I hadn't wanted to ruin her dreams of moving to the city, knowing I was rooted in Billingsley. For years, I'd always wondered if she felt the same way about me. If she felt that crackle in the air like I did every time she was near.

The day I got the invitation, I figured I had my answer. I drowned myself in a sea of whiskey, trying to convince myself it was for the best as I traced my thumb repeatedly over her gold-foiled name on the card. I was set on not coming to this damn wedding until I'd convinced myself in the final hour that I needed to get it all off my chest and tell her everything.

It's how I ended up out here in a black suit and tie, silently freaking out until she walked up. She'd just given me the opening I needed, almost like she was begging me to give her a reason to not go through with the wedding.

I wanted to give her that reason, tell her it was me she belonged with. But as I stared at her in her dress, moments away from walking down the aisle, I couldn't do it.

For all I knew, this was just a momentary freak-out for her. I wasn't going to be the one to potentially destroy her happiness, no matter how selfish I wanted to be in the moment. A sharp pain stabbed at my chest as I realized what I was about to do... It looked like her dad wouldn't be the only one giving her away today.

I reached out, brushing a stray hair from her forehead, giving her a forced smile that I hoped looked genuine as I told her the biggest lie of my life.

"Complete madness." The words were strangled as I said them. I averted my eyes as she locked onto them, hoping she couldn't see the deception there. Clearing my throat, I dropped my hand from her soft skin and tucked it safely in my pocket. "Your old man must be sneaking a few pre-game shots himself."

She nodded with a smile. She didn't seem surprised by my answer and I tried to ignore the disappointment in her eyes. "Yeah," she said, looking away from me. "Like I said, I'm just being silly. We both know we've never been more than just friends. And besides, you aren't the marrying kind anyway, right? Isn't that what you've always told me?"

There was a protective bite to her words. The way she

was suddenly lashing out at me was confusing, even if she was just repeating something I'd told her years ago when she'd returned home during a summer break from college.

She'd been giving me a hard time about the girls I was hooking up with, while she had a steady boyfriend back at school—the man she'd soon be marrying. I'd said those words to throw her off from my true feelings, and because part of me didn't want to end up like my old man and younger brother—lonely and broken from losing the only women they'd ever loved.

Mom had died when we were young, leaving my father to raise us kids on his own, and my brother, Tucker, had been devastated when his longtime girlfriend skipped town without a word. I was young and stupid at the time, I tossed those words so freely in her face, my pride and ego more important than telling Jenna that I wanted more for us than just our friendship. That same ego and pride were working their way up my spine as I straightened and stepped away from her.

Before either of us could say more, the door I'd escaped through earlier came open. Both of us turned to look as Jen's roommate from college popped her head around the corner.

"There you are! We've been looking everywhere for you!"

I took another few steps away from Jen, afraid I'd lose control of my urge to grab her and beg her to stay with me, to run away with me.

"I didn't interrupt anything, did I?" her friend, Stacy, teased, not knowing how on target she was.

"Nah," I said, winking at Stacy. "Just a few last-minute celebratory shots before our girl here ties the knot. You want to join us?"

"I wish I could, but we're being told it's go time... How about you find me later and we'll take a few of our own together," she suggested confidently with a seductive grin. Her confidence wasn't surprising; she was a cute girl.

"You can count on it, sweetheart," I said, playing the role everyone expected me to play.

Jen exaggerated the clearing of her throat. I turned to look at her once again. I wished I hadn't. That final look broke me as she told me just how she truly felt with her eyes —disappointed, angry, hurt.

She turned her back to me and walked away without another word. I panicked in that moment, her name coming out in a rush, "Jen! Wait!"

She stopped, spinning around to look at me. I froze for a split second, not knowing what the hell I was doing. I glanced between her and Stacy, realizing I needed to get control of my fucking emotions and stop falling apart like a damn pussy. They both waited for me to speak, so I said the first thing I could think of. The truth.

"I hope he makes you happy, Cricket."

Her eyes glistened with unshed tears as she nodded with a weak smile. She walked the rest of the way, meeting Stacy at the building corner, giving me one final glance over her shoulder before disappearing from my view.

I didn't stick around to watch her wedding. I didn't trust

myself to not stand up when the preacher asked if anyone objected to their union. Instead, I hauled ass out of town as fast and as far as I could from her.

1

DEVIN

Exhausted, I flopped back into the oversized, leather chair that sat behind my new desk with a heavy exhale. I surveyed my new office—unpacked boxes littered the floor, bookshelves that lined one side of the room sat empty, and the beige walls were depressingly bare. I had my work cut out for me to get this place organized. Not that I was complaining.

In fact, in no way would I ever complain about any work that was thrown my way in the future. I was lucky to have the job. Lucky to be given the chance at a fresh start—new job, new town, new house, a new life all together. It's what I needed after everything that happened.

There was a knock on my door and then a head popping through the opening as I looked toward where Dr. Hamilton stood with a huge, toothy smile. "Hope I'm not interrupting anything."

"Not at all," I said, standing to greet my new boss.

He stepped deeper into the room as he glanced around, shoving his hands in his pockets. He was dressed casually in jeans and an old, worn shirt. It looked like he'd been doing some weekend yard work before he'd shown up here unexpectedly.

"Looks like you're getting settled in okay," he observed.

"Yep. I hope that's fine. I was unpacking at the house when I came across all the boxes I wanted here at the office. Figured I'd get them all moved and put away before starting work Monday morning."

"Of course, it's okay. It's why I gave you a key to the place. Feel free to come and go as you please, Devin. I know I'm your boss for the time being, but I don't want you to think of this job as if you're just an employee. This place will all be yours one day."

I nodded, giving him an appreciative smile as he crossed the room, wrapping me in a warm hug.

Pulling back from our embrace, he bent his knees slightly to look me in the eye. "I'm glad you finally took me up on my offer, kiddo. And your aunt is, too. It means I can work less and finally have time to do some more traveling before I'm too old to jet set across the world."

"You mean, you aren't too old already?" I teased my uncle.

"Maybe so," he chuckled, "but I'm gonna pretend I'm not." He released his hold on me as he stepped away. "Besides, you're only as old as you feel, right? That makes me not a day older than forty."

I grinned, walking over to the stack of boxes. "Speaking

of working too much, what are *you* doing here on a Saturday?" I asked as I started pulling the books out of them to shove on a shelf.

"I stopped by to ask you a question, actually." He folded his hands behind his back as he rocked back onto his heels. "I tried calling your phone a few times but you didn't answer. Figured I might find you here."

"Sorry about that. I must have left my phone in the car."

I didn't tell him it was on purpose. Noah hadn't stopped calling and texting since I left Austin a few days ago. I didn't have the strength to have the same fight with him over and over, but I couldn't quite bring myself to block his number just yet.

"No worries. We just wanted to see if you'd join us for dinner Monday night. Your aunt is set on cooking you a welcome dinner. I figure it might be a thank-you-for-getting-my-husband-away-from-the-office dinner, also." His old face wore a smile as he spoke.

I laughed as I agreed. "I'd love to. I haven't had a home-cooked meal that I didn't have to make myself in months. What time should I be there?"

"Dinner is at six but feel free to come by at any time."

"Should I bring anything?" I asked over my shoulder as I placed the last few books in the box on the shelf.

"Nope. You know your Aunt Jane. She'll have it all covered."

I did know. She was just like my mom, her sister, the epitome of a southern hostess. She'd have enough food to feed an army.

"Okay. I'll bring some wine." I grinned, looking up at him from the second box I'd started to unpack.

It was his turn to chuckle, with his gray head lightly shaking, because we both knew no matter what you were told, you never showed up empty handed when invited over for dinner. "It'll be good having you around. It's been too quiet ever since Jenna married and left home."

"I'm glad to be here."

It was the honest truth. It had been a rash decision at first —made from hurt and anger—and after I'd accepted, I was second-guessing my decision to leave my job at the Austin City Zoo to become a small-town vet. But when I started to think of some of the happiest times in my life, most of them had to do with this place.

Growing up, I spent many holidays and summers here with Jenna. We'd always been close, raised more like sisters than cousins. All our summers were spent together, whether in Austin, where I was born and raised, here in Billingsley, or at the shared family lake house.

My Uncle Robert had been asking me for years to come join him at his practice. I'd turned him down every time, since the day I graduated vet school, until recently.

He smiled fondly at my response. "You need any help with all this stuff?"

"Nope. I've got it covered."

Even if I didn't, I'd figure it out. I was determined to start doing everything on my own, whether it be hanging a picture or buying a house. I was planning my life and future with only me in mind.

"Don't have to tell me twice. I'll get out of your hair. If you change your mind or need anything, don't hesitate to call or swing by the house."

"Thank you. And I will," I said, giving him a hug good-bye. Once he'd gone, I got to work unpacking and pulling my office together.

———

MY PHONE WAS STILL RINGING as I slipped into the driver's seat of my car. I glanced over at the screen lying face up in the passenger seat. If it was Noah, I was hitting ignore and turning it off for the rest of the evening.

I picked it up, smiling and relieved when I saw it wasn't. "Hey."

"Hey! Where have you been? I've been trying to reach you all day. I was starting to worry and was about to call Mom and Dad to see if they'd seen or heard from you," Jenna reprimanded.

"I've been busy unpacking. Sorry. I was actually about to call you and ask where's a good place to get a drink in this town?"

"That kind of day, huh?"

"That kind of month."

"He's not letting up, is he?"

"Nope. It's been nonstop since I packed the U-Haul and left."

"I'm sorry, Dee. The man is an idiot. He better hope I don't see him anytime soon, or he's going to be walking away as a dickless dickhead.

"I'd owe you if you made that happen."

"Consider it done. Now, enough about jackass, how are you settling in?"

"Good. I just finished at the office. I still have tons to do at the house, but figured I'd take my time with that. I'm done for the night."

"Well, if you're set on grabbing a drink somewhere, Dudley's is pretty much the only decent place in town."

I switched my phone over to my car's Bluetooth as I searched for the bar on my GPS. "Thanks."

"Don't thank me, yet. You haven't seen the place."

A small smile broke through as I turned over the ignition, steering the car out of the parking lot and in the direction of Dudley's. "I'm not picky. I'm sure it will be just what I need."

"Okay. I warned you, though. Be safe and call me if you need anything."

"I will. Later, tater."

"Bye, fry." I could hear the smile in her voice as she responded with our traditional sign-off.

I clicked 'end' and cranked up the music of The White Stripes "Seven Nation Army."

———

DUDLEY'S WASN'T as low key and empty as I expected. It seemed it wasn't the only place to be on a Saturday night but *the* place to be. When I pulled up to the metal building with nothing more than a gravel parking lot filled with haphazardly parked cars, I thought maybe my GPS had led me astray. But there was no missing the bright neon sign plastered on the side of the building.

There was a moment I considered I might be underdressed in a pair of black skinny jeans with holes at the knees, an oversized vintage Rolling Stones tee that continued to slide off my left shoulder, Chucks on my feet, and my black hair in a messy top knot with barely a stitch of makeup on my face, but then I realized I didn't care. I wasn't here to impress anybody.

I wasn't looking for a man. The last thing I needed or wanted was to be hit on. I'd prefer if I repulsed every man tonight and maybe for the foreseeable future. The only person I wanted to approach me was the bartender, and I didn't need to look good for that to happen. They were paid to serve me no matter how unattractive I might be.

As I swung the door open and stepped inside, the music came to a screeching halt and every patron in the bar fell silent as their heads spun to stare at me.

Okay. Maybe it wasn't *that* dramatic of an entrance, but it did feel like all eyes were on me as I made my way to an empty barstool. I was just waiting for an old cowboy to walk up to me and say: "You ain't from 'round here are ya?"

I was definitely underdressed compared to the other women in the bar, which was the only reason I could figure people felt the need to stare.

Note to self: Next time, I should try to blend in more if I want to draw less attention to myself.

It didn't matter at this point. I was committed and determined. I'd have a few shots and then I'd get the hell out of here. I just needed a little something to relax my muscles after all the moving and stress I'd dealt with over the last few weeks.

My phone rang once again with a call from Noah.

I sighed as I climbed onto the stool and stared down at the phone in my hand.

I wished he'd just stop. Mostly, because he was already wearing me down. At some point, I knew I'd give in and answer. Noah made me feel weak, something I wasn't proud of. I hit ignore and silenced my phone as the bartender approached.

"What's it gonna be?"

"Tequila. Fully dressed," I said, setting my phone face down on the bar.

"Coming right up," he said as he walked away. Within seconds he was back in front of me, sliding the shot glass into my hand. "You wanna keep it open?"

I tilted my head back, draining the glass of its contents before taking a bite from the lime. I waited for the distinct burn that flowed down my throat and warmed my belly to subside before responding with a nod of my head. "Yes, and I'll have another."

He returned with another shot and a glass of ice water, placing them both in front of me. I arched an eyebrow. "You cutting me off already?"

He chuckled. "Nope. Just making sure you don't get ahead of yourself."

"I can handle myself, but thanks."

"I have no doubt you can," he commented, not bothering to argue with me any further. With a grin on his face, he walked away again.

I ignored the water and took the other shot before spinning in my seat to take in the scene. A live band played cover songs on the stage across the room as the patrons milled around, lost in their own conversations, or glided across the dance floor. My eyes landed on one particular dancing couple that were playing grab ass for all to see, which made my eyes want to roll into the back of my head.

She laughed, her blond head falling to the side as he nibbled on her neck and whispered something in her ear. I felt a rolling pang in my stomach. I tried to convince myself it was from the back-to-back shots, not jealousy. I knew how being held by a man, being given that kind of attention, could make you feel. I also knew how blinded you could become by a feeling like that.

She was pretty, nothing special, but pretty. Her clothes were tight and revealing, probably helping to land her tall, tan, and handsome. Not that I was looking. Or even knew if he was truly attractive. He'd yet to remove his face from her neck for me to really know. I'd only seen his backside, which even *I* couldn't deny was nice in a pair of jeans.

As if he'd heard my thoughts, they rotated and his head lifted with a gorgeous smile, beautiful green eyes, and the most perfect face I'd ever seen. The man was sickeningly attractive.

I couldn't help staring. Not just because he was hot and what would be considered universally good-looking to even the pickiest of women, but because there was something familiar about him. I just couldn't quite recall how I might know him.

The second his eyes roamed from her face to mine, I about fell out of my seat in embarrassment from his knowing expression. He'd caught me staring. Hard.

I spun back around to face the bar, trying to find a way to distract myself from the flush I felt creeping up my skin. Catching the bartender's gaze, I signaled for another round. He took his sweet time pouring my drink.

Damn shot-blocker.

When he finally set my third shot down in front of me, a warm body slid into the seat next to me. "You can put her drink on my tab, Timmy."

Timmy, the tequila-hoarding bartender, nodded and walked off before I could object to the stranger's demand. Frustrated, I turned to face the man and tell him an obligatory thank you but was too dumbstruck to form words. Staring back at me was the man with the lethal smile, who I'd been basically eye-fucking only moments ago.

As he peered down at me, oozing confidence, words finally shot from my mouth. "I won't sleep with you."

His brows raised in question, a smirk tugging at the corner of his mouth.

"For the shot," I explained further. "I won't sleep with you just because you bought me a shot."

"It's just a shot, brown eyes. A friendly gesture with no expectations attached. Besides"—he angled his body away from me and faced the bar—"we both know that's not gonna be the reason you sleep with me." He lifted the beer in his right hand, taking a slow pull from the bottle.

I found myself unable to look away from him once again, despite his obnoxious comment. While staring at his profile, it suddenly hit me.

I know him.

Or more like, I knew *of* him. So much so that I felt like I might as well have known him personally. My mind was even more made up at that moment than it was before. This man, with his killer looks and seductive smile, was the last thing I needed in my life.

"That's where you're wrong. I won't be sleeping with you at all."

2

I lowered my beer as she spoke, a warning in her tone as her gaze sliced through me. As determined as she sounded, I could see the heat in her eyes. She wanted me, but she wasn't going to make it easy.

It was nice to know she held herself to a higher standard. Most of the women around here hardly ever made it a chase. That alone made her even more attractive to me than I'd already thought she was the moment my eyes found her.

She was a natural beauty—dark, raven-colored hair, beautiful light brown eyes, a tight, petite figure with just enough curves to grab onto, and full lips. I wanted to do dirty things with that mouth. The same mouth that was frowning at me now.

"You got a name, brown eyes?"

"Doesn't everybody?"

I cracked a smile as I stifled a laugh. This woman was

definitely different from what I was used to. A challenge. I liked a good challenge. Yet, something about her smart mouth and laid-back confidence was familiar.

Switching from watching me to keeping her eyes straight ahead, she took her shot of tequila like a champ then signaled for another. When I looked over at Timmy, I saw his hesitance. I didn't blame him after counting the number of empty shot glasses in front of her. She'd already had three in what had to be less than thirty minutes. I gave him a silent signal, letting him know not to worry. I'd make sure she got home safe if she ended up drunk as hell.

I could see him release a heavy sigh as his shoulders deflated. He shook his head in defeat while reaching for another glass and the bottle of tequila.

"A woman of mystery. Is that what you're going for?"

"No. I'm just not interested. Besides, aren't you here with somebody?"

"Jealous?"

She scoffed a sarcastic laugh, shaking her head. "You should leave me alone and go find her. I'm sure she'd be happy to finish what you started on the dance floor."

"So, you've been keeping an eye on me," I goaded.

She rolled her eyes and took a sip of her water.

"She's in the ladies' room and I'm sure you're right. But she's not the one I want to talk to right now," I added.

She turned to look at me once again, her eyes nothing more than thin slits. "So, what was your plan here, slick? Get my number while she drained her bladder and was none the wiser?"

I gritted my teeth at her comment, my muscles tensing. I could handle someone busting my balls, even a stranger like herself who knew nothing about me. I didn't give a rat's ass what most people thought of me. My family's and close friends' opinions were the only ones that mattered.

Contrary to what most people would think, I didn't treat women badly. I respected them and didn't use them any more than they used me. If I got the hint that any woman wasn't on the same page, I'd let them down easy and walk away without taking things further. They all knew up front where I stood whenever they entered my bed. I was *not* a relationship man. At one time, I thought I might be, but that ship sailed nearly a decade ago.

And Mandy, the blonde she was trying to throw in my face, was on the same page as me. We didn't come here together, and I didn't plan on leaving here with her either. We'd shared a dance, one she initiated, and that was it. I admit, we may have gotten a little too friendly on the dance floor, more on her part than mine, but I'd already told her tonight wasn't happening.

I was here with some buddies for a guys' night out. I'd planned to return to our table after my dance with Mandy, but as soon as I saw this girl, my feet started carrying me to her. I wanted to know who the hell she was and what she was doing here all alone.

With the bite laced in every word she spoke, I was afraid I had my answer. She'd been burned. And from the looks of it, badly. It's what had me grinding my teeth to bite back the anger I was feeling, an odd protectiveness for a woman I didn't know. It was that fact I used to remind myself this wasn't my fight. It didn't seem to fucking matter.

I ignored her ridiculous accusations. "Who was it, brown eyes? Who hurt you?"

Her eyes flicked away momentarily, a sadness flashing across her face before she schooled all her features as a shield. Her lips flattened into a hard line as she refused to answer me.

I leaned in closer, poising our mouths only inches apart as I stared into her eyes. I could feel the warmth radiating off her body, hear the hitch of her breath even with the loud noise of the bar surrounding us. "Whoever it was, didn't deserve you."

"You know nothing about me." Her words were weak, nearly a whisper, paling against the strength she had before.

"You're right. I don't. And you know nothing about me. But that doesn't mean I don't recognize the pain you're trying to drown in a bottle of tequila. The same pain you're carrying and wielding as a sword against all mankind." I pulled back and reached for a cocktail napkin and a pen that had been left on top of a receipt. "I'm not him, sweetheart," I added, my eyes focused on the phone number I was scribbling onto the napkin.

Her eyes dropped, watching my hand as I slid it across the bar top to her and stood.

"I don't want your number."

"Good. Because I didn't give it to you. If you get too fucked up to drive, call that number. It's the closest thing you'll get to an Uber around here."

I turned my back to her and walked away.

"I'm just supposed to trust you? How do I know this isn't some creep?"

Turning back to look at her, I continued to back away. "When it's the right person, trust can be a beautiful thing, brown eyes." I winked and gave her my biggest damn smile before spinning once again and heading for the table where all my friends sat.

As I retook my seat next to Billy, they all tried to pretend they weren't watching us the whole damn time. They all knew me well enough to read the look on my face and keep their mouths shut.

———

I SWIPED to answer my phone as I took the steps two at a time up to my front porch. "Hey, buddy."

"What the hell? I don't have the patience for this, man," Roger growled on the other end.

"Is that the bastard? You tell him I want to talk to him!"

Oh, now she wants to talk. I chuckled as I heard the slur in her angry voice in the background.

There was some shuffling as Roger's voice became distant. "Lady, if you don't cut that shit out, I'll arrest you and throw you in the back of the car."

I imagined he was fighting to hold onto his phone.

"You can't do that," she hissed.

"I can, and I will. You ever hear of assaulting a police officer, or public intoxication? I can arrest you on both counts if

I want. So, keep your hands on that side of the car and pipe down."

I bit my fist, trying not to bust out laughing at their muffled conversation. It sounded like she was giving my buddy Roger hell already.

When I'd taken off from Dudley's for the night, she'd still been planted at the bar, scaring off any man who dared approach her. And there were plenty who did. As I closed out my tab and covered hers, I let Timmy know I'd given her Roger's number. He agreed to call him if she didn't do it on her own. I wasn't sure if she'd called him, but she sure as hell didn't sound happy about being in his squad car, so my guess was Timmy did it for her.

"You all right over there, Roger?"

"No! I'm not okay! Your lady friend here is a real pain in the ass."

"I'm not one of his lady friends! He only wishes!" she yelled in the background again.

He ignored her as he continued to chew me out. "You can't keep using me as your personal car service, asshole. You're gonna get my ass fired."

"First of all, your dad is your boss. He's not gonna fire you. And what did you expect me to do? Let her drive home drunk?"

"Why couldn't you take her?"

"Do you not hear her screaming next to you? She's not my biggest fan." At least, not at the moment. I was hoping to change that in the future.

"You owe me, dick wad."

I knew he'd forgive me. It's not that he's a pushover. We'd just been friends for years. He'd always been there for me and I for him.

"Thanks, man. And I promise. Never again."

"Yeah, right," he scoffed. "I'll talk to you later."

"Good luck, buddy."

The line died with her screaming at Roger to not hang up. I shook my head, laughing to myself as I walked inside my house. I had a good feeling I'd be dreaming about a smart-mouthed, black-haired beauty tonight.

———

LOTTIE WAS ALREADY RUSHING out her front door with my baby nephew in tow before I could even park my truck. I jumped out and met her at the bottom step.

"Thank you so much for coming, Wes. I've been worried sick and not sure what to do, with Tucker gone and Billy with Hannah at her OB appointment."

I took the baby carrier hooked on her arm, helping to carry it over to her car. As frazzled as she sounded, she still managed to look put-together, with her fancy clothes and auburn hair perfectly styled. "Don't mention it, Lottie. We're family. It's what we do. Where is she?"

"In the barn. She won't eat. Doesn't even seem interested."

"You call Dr. Hamilton?" I asked as I passed her back the carrier and she locked it into place in the backseat of her car.

"Yes. His office said he'd be stuck in surgery with the

Winkelmans' boxer most of the day, but he'd stop by as soon as he could. If I had anyone else to cover the store today, I'd stay with her and wait."

"Dolly will be fine. I'll keep an eye on her until he shows up. You focus on taking care of business."

I bent down, giving Colton a smile and a baby hand-shake. "Hey there, little man. Tell your mama, Uncle Wes has it under control and not to worry." He babbled at me with a cute fucking smile and I winked, grinning back at him before standing upright and closing the door. Normally, I'd spend a lot more time playing with the little guy, but it was obvious she was in a rush to drop him at Grams' so she could get to work.

She hugged me, lifting to her toes to kiss me on the cheek. "You're a saint. I don't care what Tuck says about you," she teased as I opened the driver's door of her car.

She slid into the leather seat and I shut her door. After starting the car, she rolled down her window. I bent down so we were eye level.

"You'll call me if things change, if she gets worse?"

Worry was written all over her face. Dolly had been her mom's horse. After losing her mom, I knew she'd held onto Dolly as a way to hold onto a piece of her mother. If Dolly didn't pull through whatever this was, it would devastate my sister-in-law, and my niece, who'd also grown attached to the old mare.

"I promise."

She nodded, a weak smile on her face.

"Go on, now. Grams is waiting on you two."

She didn't waste another second before taking off down the dirt road of her family farm. I headed straight to the barn to check on Dolly and wait for Dr. Hamilton to show. Unfortunately, that meant I'd have nothing but time on my hands. And in the last thirty-eight hours, whenever I had time on my hands, that led to me trying to figure out who the woman from the bar was Saturday night.

It shouldn't be that hard, with the way this town gossiped. But for some reason, I hadn't heard a damn thing about any new girl in town. I'd even asked Grams last night at Sunday dinner. She'd said she didn't know...but something told me she did and just wasn't telling me. Maybe it was the smirk on her face she was trying to hide, or the mischievous twinkle in her eye that usually meant she was up to something.

It didn't matter. I'd find out soon enough. A girl like that wouldn't go unnoticed for long in this town.

3

DEVIN

he Monroes. When my Uncle Robert said he needed me to make a house call earlier this morning to visit my first patient, I was thrilled. Especially when I found out it was a horse. My favorite animal on this earth. Then he'd said the owners' name. *The Monroes.*

I may not be from Billingsley, but I knew enough to know just who the Monroes were, and what sort of influence they had in this town. How they owned most of the land surrounding its city limits. How they were a beloved family in these parts, all of them charming and good-looking. How one of them had been my cousin's closest childhood friend until the day she'd married. And based on my reaction to the news—eyes wide, mouth slightly agape—my uncle realized I had some idea too.

"Not *that* Monroe." Uncle Robert had grinned, knowingly.

What he didn't know was, I'd already had a run-in with *that* Monroe the other night. The oldest of the two brothers. The heir to more than half of the Monroe estate, only because the younger brother had chosen a different career path for his life. Word on the street was Tucker Monroe now owned a very successful construction company.

"You'll need to drive out to the Davis farm. Tina has the address for you at the front desk," he'd told me before heading into another surgery on the Winkelmans' boxer. Apparently, this was the third time the dog had swallowed one of their kids' Nerf balls this year.

I turned off the main road that led from town to Monroe territory onto a long, dirt drive lined with large live oaks forming a canopy overhead. They were the only trees for miles, the rest of the land covered in crops. The tunnel of trees ended, and the sky opened up to a quaint little farmhouse and old, red barn.

I slowed my car to a stop, glad I had the forethought to stop at my place on the way and change from my skirt and heels to jeans. I reached into my backseat, grabbing my medical kit before stepping out of the car. Gravel crunched under my boots as I took a few steps and glanced around, wondering if I should knock on the front door or head straight to the barn.

When I saw movement from the corner of my eye near the barn-door opening, I turned that direction with a smile on my face, ready to introduce myself to Lottie Monroe. Only, it wasn't a woman standing in the barn with eyes glued to my body, doing a thorough sweep. It was a man. My smile fell as I cursed under my breath.

"Well, hey there, brown eyes," Wes Monroe drawled, crossing his arms over his broad chest with a sly smile on his face. "I knew you'd realize you couldn't resist me sooner or later."

Immediately, I wondered if this was nothing but a trick. I wouldn't put it past him after the other night. "What are you doing here?"

"I could ask you the same thing."

My head tilted to the side as I glared at him, planting one hand on my hip while my other tightened around the handle of my bag. I wasn't sure what kind of game he was playing, but interfering with my job, wasting my time, was not gonna fly.

"You're a real piece of work, you know that?"

He started to speak with that annoying smile on his face, but I cut him off.

"First, you called the sheriff on me the other night—"

"Technically, I didn't—"

"And now this. This isn't a game. This is my job. You can't just pretend to have a sick horse to prank me into coming all the way out here." I ended my tirade, turning away and stomping back toward my car.

"Whoa, now. Calm down, sweetheart." His hand was suddenly gripping my elbow, spinning me to face him. "I think you're getting the wrong idea. I didn't call you here. Lottie did."

"Lottie? Right," I snapped. "You sure don't look like a Lottie."

"And you sure as hell don't look like Dr. Hamilton," he pointed out.

My mouth opened and closed—twice—understanding hitting me smack in the face. I wiggled my arm from his grasp, embarrassment replacing my previous anger, knowing I'd overreacted.

"I'm sorry," I said, taking a step back, needing some space as I got control of my angry breathing. He was crowding me, and the addictive scent he was wearing was making me irrational. At least, that was my excuse. Logical or not.

"Don't worry about it." He grinned with adorable eyes, rubbing at the back of his neck. He glanced at the field over my head before refocusing his eyes on me. "How about we start over?"

"How about you show me the horse?" I countered. As badly as I felt about my outburst, my decision to keep him at a distance hadn't changed.

His grin turned into a knowing smile. "Sure. Right this way." He held out his arm, allowing me to lead the way back to the barn.

I could feel his eyes on me as I walked. I kept my shoulders back and head high, refusing to let it affect me. As we walked inside, his fingers landed on the curve of my back, causing me to jolt a little at the unexpected contact.

He leaned in, brushing his lips dangerously close to the sensitive spot near my ear, intensifying the warm tingles that radiated from where his hand still lingered. "This way," the low gravel of his voice demanded.

I forced myself not to react any more than I already had. The man was cocky enough. His hand fell from my body as he walked ahead of me to open the stall door, and I hated to admit I kind of wished he was still touching me.

"My name is Wes, by the way," he called over his shoulder, glancing back at me as he wiggled the latch. When I didn't respond, he shook his head with a light chuckle at my intentional silence. "I'm not sure where you come from, brown eyes, but here, it's customary to tell someone *your* name when they introduce themselves to you." He pulled the door open.

I ignored him, again. Partly, because I knew it was driving him crazy that I hadn't told him my name, but also because all my focus was suddenly drawn to the horse he'd brought me to see.

"She's beautiful. What's her name?" I asked, stepping inside the stall. I set my bag on the ground, but kept my distance from her for the moment.

"Dolly."

"Is she yours?"

He shook his head. "No. My sister-in-law's... She originally belonged to Lottie's mom, but she passed away a few years back. Now, she belongs to Lottie. My niece, Lily, is the one who rides her mostly, though."

I listened to him talk as I watched Dolly slam her front left hoof in the dirt, repeatedly pawing at the ground, grunting with irritable movements. "Has she been acting this restless for long?"

He nodded. "A day or so. It started about the same time she stopped eating. We thought maybe it was just a mild case of colic, but Lottie didn't want to take any chances."

"Any changes in her diet?" I asked, reaching out for her now, letting her get a whiff of my palm before running my hand down over the white spot on her forehead. "Good girl, Dolly," I whispered to her as I continued to brush my hand along the short hairs of her brown coat. "Don't worry, we'll get you feeling better in no time."

I looked over my shoulder at Wes when he didn't immediately answer. He shook his head, as if in a daze, before finally responding.

"No. She's been eating the same food we've been giving her for years. Same as all the other horses. None of them seem to be having any issues."

"What about her water intake?"

He rubbed at his neck. "I don't think she's drinking much now."

"How often does she get turned out?"

"At least twice a day. Some days, depending on the weather, we let them stay out there all day."

I nodded, turning my attention back to Dolly, giving her a few more pats before I walked over to my bag. Opening it, I pulled out my stethoscope and a pair of gloves. Wes stood quietly off to the side, his hands in his front pockets, as I took her pulse rate.

After checking her pulse, I placed my hand over her

muzzle to feel the air flow and check her respiratory rate. He continued to watch me closely as I took her temperature, checked her gums, and gave her an overall look, physically. Every time I tried to discreetly peek at him, our eyes would catch. He'd grin, and I'd quickly turn my attention back to Dolly, clearing my throat to ask more questions as my belly fluttered.

Feeling nervous was ridiculous. It was a routine check. One an intern could do. I was an experienced vet. And a good one. When it came to my career, I didn't lack any confidence in my capabilities. But I refused to acknowledge the other reason I might feel nervous as I worked. Why *he* might make me feel nervous.

Wes Monroe being anything more than an acquaintance was out of the question. I'd been burned enough by men like him. And then there was the whole Jenna factor.

"Well, what do you think?" he asked, stepping closer to me, running his hand over Dolly's neck and down, where it brushed against mine.

The light touch had my tummy doing another flip. A slow smile built on his face as I quickly pulled my hand away from Dolly, putting some space back between us. "It could be colic..."

"But you don't think it is?" His face switched to concern.

"I think there's more to it. You said there were no changes in her diet, right? She hasn't gotten into anything out of the norm?"

"No. At least, not that I know of." He lifted his cap, methodically scratching at the back of his head.

I sighed, my brows pulling inward as I processed everything. All signs and symptoms pointed to colic...except her
gums were a darker shade of red than I typically liked to
see... "Are those oak trees lining the road as I drove in?"

"Yeah. Why?"

"Any chance she'd have been over by them? Maybe eaten
a couple acorns?"

"Shit"—he replaced his cap, running a hand over the
scruff on his jaw—"Lily likes to ride her up and down the
road. She must have let her eat them, not knowing. We never
told her not to."

"Well, I'd still like to run a few lab tests, just to be
safe. I'll get a few swab samples to take back. In the mean-
time, could you ask your niece if she did? That would
help narrow down the possibilities. I'm also worried Dolly
may already be getting dehydrated. I'm going to admin-
ister IV fluid therapy and some active charcoal over the
next few hours. I don't want to take any chances, since
that seems the most probable cause. Between the red
gums, colic, and dehydration, they all point to some kind
of poisoning. I can give her some painkillers for the colic,
also."

"Will she be okay?"

"As long as there's no severe kidney damage, yes. She
should be able to recover in the next sixty days. I suggest you
remove any acorn or oak debris as soon as possible. Even
though they are poisonous to them, horses can still develop a
taste for them, and it will be a dangerous on-going problem
for her if that's the case."

"Of course, I'll make sure Billy takes care of it today. And I'll talk to Lily about keeping her away from there."

"What's that?" Another male voice I didn't recognize asked from behind me.

I turned to look at the very-good-looking man who'd appeared just inside the barn. He walked the rest of the distance to us, stopping and shaking Wes's hand.

"Hey, what are you doing here? I thought Hannah had an appointment."

"Yep. Already went and took her home to rest. Just stopped by to see how Dolly was doing before I got to work. Lottie said she still wasn't acting right."

"Yeah. We're thinking acorn poisoning. We need to get the road cleaned up today."

"Shit. Of course." The man nodded, turning to look at me. "I'm Billy Miller"—he smiled, offering his hand—"I work for the Monroes, helping out on both farms. So, I guess that makes Wes here my boss."

"And his wife's BFF. He forgot that part," Wes chimed in, leaning over my shoulder.

Billy rolled his eyes. "He's not."

"I am," Wes insisted with a grin. "He just can't stand that I am."

We both ignored Wes.

"Nice to meet you, Billy. Dr. Devin Chaplin." I returned his smile, taking off a glove and shaking his hand. "And that's unfortunate you have to deal with him daily." I jutted my thumb in Wes' direction.

Billy chuckled, dropping my hand.

"What the hell?" Wes huffed from behind me. "You'll tell Miller your name but not me?"

"You're standing there with two capable ears, aren't you?" I retorted, glancing over my shoulder at him.

"Wait. You're the new vet, then," Billy said, his smile widening. "I heard in town this morning Dr. Hamilton had brought on a new vet. His niece, right?"

"Yep. That would be me," I said, mildly.

"His niece? As in, Jen's cousin?" Wes asked, his face paling as he looked at me as if he was seeing me for the first time. I had no doubt he was connecting all the dots, realizing our shared connection the way I had the other night.

"That's normally how the family tree works," I grumbled as I stepped back toward Dolly, petting the side of her neck.

"Wow. *Jenna*. I haven't seen her in years. How is she?" Billy inquired, crossing his arms over his chest.

"I'm gonna head out," Wes snapped before I could respond. His whole demeanor had changed, his playful smile from earlier gone and replaced with a hard glare as he looked at me. He turned away, directing all his attention to Billy. "I need to get back to the farm to help Dad. Can you finish things up here with Dr. Chaplin?"

"Uh...yeah, sure," Billy agreed, his face twisting in confusion.

Wes didn't bother saying good-bye to either of us. He walked straight out of the barn without so much as a wave, a smile, or even one of his damn winks.

Billy looked from Wes' retreating backside to me and

shrugged, as if the sudden change in his boss was of no concern.

I took off my other glove, laying the pair on my bag as I struggled with the now-awkward silence. "Umm...I just need to grab some supplies from my car. I'll be right back," I announced, rushing out of the barn.

I was surprised to see Wes hadn't peeled out of there yet. He stood silently at his truck, fists gripping the edge of the tailgate, his head lowered between his muscular arms as he stared at the ground.

I hesitated to continue the trek to my car, unsure if I should just turn around and hide until he was gone. But my chance to flee vanished when his head lifted to look at me.

He stood upright, his tall frame tense and intimidating. "You knew who I was the other night when we met at the bar," he accused.

I nodded, knowing there was no sense in denying the truth. "Not at first, but soon after you sat down. I recognized you from some old pictures...and, well, that one summer when we were all about seven years old. We'd met briefly."

"I see..." He nodded his head, walking away. He gripped the handle of the driver's door. "So, who's the one playing games now, Doc?"

My whole body tensed with regret. He didn't give me a chance to respond or defend myself. He climbed in his truck, slamming the door and peeling out on the dirt road, just as I'd expected.

———

I SPENT the rest of my afternoon with Dolly, administering her fluids and meds over the course of a few hours. I prayed I wasn't too late in giving her the medical attention she needed. I'd called into the office, letting them know where I'd be. Uncle Robert sent our technician to retrieve the swab samples from me, so he could start running the labs.

Lottie had stopped by the barn when she arrived home. It was obvious how much the horse meant to her. Not only was I immediately growing attached to Dolly, the way I always tended to do with my animal patients, but I instantly hit it off with Lottie. I wanted to be able to tell her everything would be okay with her horse.

Part of me wondered if I'd see Wes again that day. But after the coldness I felt when he walked away, I was pretty sure he no longer wanted anything to do with me. It was all for the best, I reminded myself.

By the time I left the Davis farm, I was too exhausted to even eat. Instead, I wanted to take a long, hot shower, have a cup of hot chamomile tea, and crash while reading a book. Unfortunately, I'd already promised to have dinner with my aunt and uncle. It looked like a bottle of wine and a pan of Aunt Jane's brownies were going to have to do.

———

I TOOK a deep inhale of the crisp fall air as I strolled down the town square sidewalk, headed for Ida's. Uncle Robert had brought in a box of cinnamon rolls for the office on Tuesday morning. I swore with the first bite, it was like heaven had landed in my mouth.

I'd made myself wait until today, Thursday, before I allowed myself to give into my craving for another one. I was a junky for junk food. It's why I had to be careful about how often I ate it. Sugar loved to stick to my pre-existing curves. I was shorter than most on top of it all, a family trait. If I wasn't careful about what I ate and religious about my workouts, I'd end up looking like a bowling ball.

The door chimed as I entered, and the sweet smells of warm, fresh pastries and freshly brewed coffee filled the air as I walked into Ida's. There was a short line of heads in front of me, one of which I recognized. There was no missing Lottie's beautiful red hair. The woman was gorgeous. I had no doubt her and Tucker's offspring were going to break millions of hearts one of these days.

Taking her to-go cup from the young kid working the register, she smiled and thanked him before she turned and saw me.

"Dr. Chaplin! Hey!"

"Mrs. Monroe, so nice to see you. How's Dolly?"

She fluttered her one free hand at me as she smiled. "Please, call me Lottie. And she's doing better. Still not a hundred percent, but she's getting there."

I grinned. "Feel free to call me Devin, too. And I'm glad to hear it. I was planning to make a trip out there next week to check up on her."

Lottie was someone I hoped to become friends with. We'd both been city girls at one point, who'd chosen to move to Billingsley for our own happiness. Her move had a lot to do with finding happiness with her husband, Tucker. Mine, on the other hand, was to escape the man I'd fallen for. Regardless, we could somewhat relate to each other.

"Great. Let me know when, and I'll make sure to have Hannah cover the shop, so I can be there this time."

I'd learned during our previous conversation that Lottie co-owned the only fashionable boutique in town with her friend, Hannah Miller. I'd done a little window shopping the other day as I passed by on my way to Ida's for a coffee. After tons of things caught my eye, I'd planned on stopping in there to check everything out up close.

"Will do."

"Okay. Well, I'll see you around!" She waved as she exited through the front door.

I waved in return, then turned back to face the front of the line, eyeing the fresh pan of cinnamon rolls being brought out from the kitchen. My mouth drooled as my stomach growled. I was so focused on the cinnamon rolls, I didn't even think twice when I reached for my phone, answering it without looking.

"Hello."

"Dev... You answered."

Every muscle in my body tensed as his voice hit my ear. *Noah. Shit.*

"It was an accident. Good-bye."

"Don't hang up! Please! Just talk to me."

"We have nothing to talk about," I bowed my head with a sigh, frustrated at myself for being too weak to hang up.

"That's not true, Devin. We can work this out. I told you I was sorry. I made a mistake. You can't just throw years together away."

"Really? *A mistake?*" I spat, clutching the phone tighter, my heart rate and body temperature rising with every word he spoke. "Was the first time you screwed her at your office the mistake, or the hundredth time you did it in your apartment? Where I found you with your head between her legs! Maybe the mistake you're actually referring to is getting caught!"

The bakery fell silent as all eyes turned to me. I snapped my mouth shut, ending the call as a heated blush spread over my face. I turned on my heels and ran out the door as fast as I could, sans cinnamon roll and coffee. Slipping down an alleyway, I heaved myself against the side of a brick building as I caught my breath and tried to cool my anger—anger at Noah for what he did, and at myself for being the victim and allowing him to get to me to the point of a public outburst.

The phone in my hand rang again. Seeing Noah's name on the screen, I gripped it firmer, refraining from chucking it across the alley and into a wall. That's when the tears of anger started to streak down my cheeks.

Why can't he just leave me alone? This was all his doing. He's the one who threw away our years together, the one who pissed on our future like it meant nothing.

I shut off my phone when it rang for a third time, dropping it into my purse and my face into my palms as I leaned against the wall.

A few feet away, a door came open and the chatter of two

women filtered through the rear exit as they stepped into the alley. *Great.* All I needed was to embarrass myself in front of a few more people. I pulled away from the wall, straightening quickly as I wiped the tears from my cheeks.

"Devin?" Lottie's voice called in surprise.

"Are you okay?" asked the other woman, who, based on her very pregnant belly, I assumed was Hannah.

"Uh, yeah. I'm fine... Sorry. I just...I got a little turned around, I guess. Low blood sugar or something making me loopy..." I was spurting out a bunch of nonsense. "I'm just gonna..." I pointed in the direction behind me with my thumb.

The two exchanged a silent look as I spun to leave.

"Devin, wait!" Lottie hollered, breaking out in a fast pace toward me. "Hey, are you sure you're okay?" she asked softly, her expression full of sympathy as she neared me.

"Yeah. Just had a rough morning, that's all."

"Okay." She bit her lip as she studied me. "So, I meant to ask you before and it just completely slipped my mind... Hannah, Leighton, and I get together every other Friday for a little girls' night. Would you want to join us tomorrow night? It's pretty low-key. We usually just take turns hosting dinner, drinking wine, and complaining about anything and every-thing," she teased.

"Sounds...perfect." I snorted a laugh, rubbing at my runny nose.

"Great! It's my turn to host. See you around seven at my place?"

"I'll be there." I gave her a weak smile.

"Okay, see ya then!" With another wave, she took off back toward Hannah, who was also smiling and waving at me. I waved back and then slipped around the corner, choosing not to take the chance of any more public humiliation, and headed straight for the office.

4

I should have known. From the moment I saw her, I should have fucking known. Once I did, it was so damn obvious.

Devin and Jenna.

Cousins.

Shit.

Any thoughts I had about Devin and me went up in flames the moment I realized. I wasn't going down that twisted road. I was smart enough to know it was a disaster waiting to happen. Jenna and I may never have been an actual item, but there were feelings there at one time, whether we acted on them or not.

Yet, knowing all of that. I couldn't get Devin Chaplin out of my mind. I'd spent all week battling thoughts of her and how she looked in those tight jeans she wore as she worked with Dolly.

She was confident. Smart. Sexy. Feisty as hell. Drawing me into her web like a black widow.

I opened my list of contacts on my phone, knowing exactly what I needed to get my mind straight. Without thought, I typed out a quick text to Mandy. She responded immediately. I smirked. She was always on board for a good time. I slipped my phone back into my pocket, feeling lighter already as Billy's truck rolled to a stop outside the tractor barn, where I'd been waiting for him to show up.

We'd been up since daybreak working to get one of the tractors fixed, the oldest one in our fleet. It was setting us back on getting the remainder of the fields plowed and ready for our fall sowing. If we couldn't get it up and running by this afternoon, we'd be working double time using the other running tractors to stay on schedule.

I glanced at the nonexistent watch on my wrist. "'Bout time you got back."

Billy frowned as he pulled the box of new parts from his backseat. "If you got a problem with how long I take, you can go into town yourself next time," he stated, passing the bags of hydraulic oil to me as I made it to his side. "At least then I don't have to listen to all the damn gossip coming out of Mrs. Adams' mouth while her old man takes his sweet time getting everything rung up."

I lightly shook my head, stifling a laugh. That was exactly why I'd sent Billy to town in the first place. Mrs. Adams was one of the main players in what we liked to call the Billingsley gossip squad. I think they believed it was their duty to spread rumors like wildfire. Any time you stepped foot in Adams Tractor Supply, you knew you were going to get an earful from his wife as Mr. Adams retrieved your online orders from the stock room.

"Who's the poor headline victim today?"

"Trust me. You don't want to know."

He was probably right. I tried to stay clear of the town gossip. Nothing good ever came from it; I knew that from personal experience. For generations now, my family had been the focus of more than their fair share of it.

I set the oil on the workbench and picked up a wrench, getting to work on installing the new parts. The old Ford tractor had seen better days. If it were solely up to me, I'd replace it with a newer model that didn't cause us any problems. I was sick of repairing it every damn year, but my old man refused to part with it and buy a new one. And you didn't argue with Beau Monroe...at least, not when it came to how to run the family farm.

The few times I'd mentioned it, he got fired up, grumbling on and on about how the new tractors weren't worth a damn, with their stupid technology, and how at least with this one we still had the right to fix it on our own. He refused to buy another new one until we had no other choice.

"So, Dr. Chaplin is pretty hot, huh?"

My hand stilled, gripping the wrench handle tighter at the mention of Devin, and the fact that Billy had been checking her out. I lightly shook my head, annoyed with myself and Billy, not sure where the hell his comment had come from. "Aren't you happily married with a baby on the way?" I asked as I started cranking the wrench again.

"Yeah. Doesn't make me blind."

"Think Hannah would appreciate your wandering eyes?"

He chuckled. "Hannah and Lottie were the ones who brought it up the other night. Seems they have it in their heads the two of you would make the perfect couple."

The wrench slipped from my hand and clattered to the concrete floor. I glared over my shoulder at Billy, who stood there with a cocky expression on his face, his arms crossed over his chest. I bent down and picked up the wrench, every muscle in my body tense.

"Well, you can tell them it's not gonna happen." I turned back to the tractor, tightening the last bolt.

Billy laughed out loud this time as he walked over to hand me a bottle of the oil.

"What?" I growled.

"Nothing, man." He shook his head with more silent laughter.

"Don't get all shy on me now, Miller. You got something to say, say it."

Hands up, palms facing out, he took a few steps back. "Just funny coming from you is all. Never seen you turn down the chance to hook up with a cute girl like her."

"I passed up on Hannah, didn't I?"

His face went straight. "Fuck you, man. Don't even go there."

It was my turn to laugh out loud. The man made it too easy. It seemed even after all this time, it still drove him nuts thinking about the time he assumed Hannah and I had hooked up.

"Relax, Miller." I grinned, glad my little jab had succeeded in shutting him up about Devin. "Get me that other bottle of fluid will ya?"

He passed it off and we both gladly moved on to conversations about the upcoming football games happening this weekend.

———————

I WALKED out of Tucker and Lottie's barn after checking in on Dolly, headed for their house to make sure Lottie didn't need anything. Tucker had been gone all week on an out-of-town job and wasn't expected back until tomorrow. I'd promised him I'd look after everything in his absence. None of us had been prepared for Dolly to get so sick.

I shot him a quick text to let him know she was looking better already. I had to admit, without Devin's perceptiveness and quick action, things might have turned out a whole lot different. None of us ever would have figured Dolly had been fed acorns. Poor Lily felt terrible and cried on my shoulder. She'd thought she'd been giving Dolly a harmless treat.

I knocked on the screen door as I let myself in, already grinning at the loud, boisterous laughter of Lottie, Hannah, and Leighton streaming down the hall from the kitchen.

Lottie was the first one to notice me, and her lips curved up as she tucked herself under my arm, giving me a side hug. "What are you doing here?"

"Just came to check on Dolly and give Tuck an update."

"On me or the horse?"

"Both." I winked, dropping my arm from her shoulders. "And it looks like you ladies are up to no good," I added, surveying the numerous bottles of wine and excessive amount of food covering every inch of the island.

"It's girls' night," Leighton filled me in.

"Which means"—Hannah slapped at my hand as I reached for a black olive off the veggie platter—"you're not invited."

"Calm down, preggers. I'm not gonna eat them all. I'll save you a few."

She glared at me and I grinned back at her, snatching one and popping it into my mouth before she could stop me this time. Riling Hannah up would never get old. And despite what she might lead everyone to believe, she loved it.

"Where are the kids?" I asked, turning back to Lottie. "I wanted to hang out with them for a bit before I headed out for the night."

"Sorry. I already dropped them at Grams' for an overnight stay. You'll have to stop by there if you want to see them."

"Sounds like you gals have a crazy night ahead of you."

"You know it. Pasta and wine with a woman who's thirty-five weeks pregnant. Doesn't get any crazier than that," Leighton poked at Hannah.

I laughed. "What's your problem?" I asked a disgruntled Leighton.

"Just ignore her," Lottie instructed. "She's just mad because she wants to go to the bar and she was overruled."

"I see. Well, ladies"—I kissed the top of Lottie's head

before moving on to Leighton and Hannah, doing the same —"I'm out. You girls be safe and don't do anything I wouldn't do."

"Well that leaves the options wide open for us, doesn't it?" Hannah teased.

I chuckled as I walked back down the hall and out the front door. I was still grinning, my eyes down as I hurried down the front steps, bumping right into a small figure.

"Shit." I grabbed her arms, keeping her from falling. "Sorry, I didn't see you there."

I dropped my hands from her body as I looked down at Devin, a bottle of wine in her hand and a nervous smile on her face. She was dressed casually again, the same way she had been the first night I met her. It was obvious she had no idea how sexy she looked like that, with nothing on but jeans, a pair of worn Chucks, and a plain T-shirt. The only difference tonight was her long, dark hair was down around her shoulders in loose curls, and she had on the smallest trace of makeup, bringing out her natural beauty.

"Where you off to in a rush? Hot date?" she joked, her voice wavering slightly despite her effort to hide her nerves. Her smile faded quickly as she caught the expression on my face.

"Would it matter if I was?"

I hadn't meant to sound so cold. But the girl got under my skin like no other, with just her presence. Plus, the truth that had been unraveled earlier in the week, and that I still wanted her despite it, irritated the hell out of me.

She took a step back, shaking her head with a frown. "I'm

sorry, Wes. I wasn't trying to deceive you. Or play games with you. I hope you believe me. I'd like us to start over. As friends."

Friends.

A humorless laugh erupted from my mouth as I pushed past her. "Go inside, Doc. There's nothing out here for you."

I didn't bother looking back at her, no matter how badly I wanted to. I didn't want to be *friends* with Devin. As much as I hated to admit it, I didn't think I could handle it. It was best for both of us if we avoided each other altogether. Problem was, it was a damn small town.

Plus, after my earlier conversation with Billy, it seemed like the few women I kept close in my life were going to make it even harder for that to happen. They were like a dog with a bone when they got ideas in their pretty little heads. That Devin was here now only proved my worst fear. It looked like I was going to have to set them all straight, before they started putting their noses where they didn't belong.

———

THE DELICIOUS SMELL of homemade chili and freshly baked cornbread entered my nose, making my stomach growl as I walked through the screen door of Grams' house.

Grams and Lily were seated around the dinner table. While Lily rambled on excitedly about her day at school, Colton slept in his swing in the corner of the room. As soon as Lily caught sight of me, she was up and running, squealing my name.

I scooped her up in my arms, spinning her around. "Hey, Lily pad. How's my favorite girl?"

She giggled as I tickled her side. "What are you doing here?"

"Came to see you. I missed you." I kissed her cheek, setting her back on her feet.

"You saw me yesterday," she reminded me.

I ruffled her brown, curly hair, walking beside her to the table. "Doesn't matter. I always miss you when you're not around."

"I'm sure you say that to all the girls," she sighed audibly, her eyes rolling. She took her seat, digging into her bowl of chili, completely oblivious to the sharp stab her words just delivered to my heart.

Grams stifled a laugh and I arched an eyebrow at her. "Sounds like Aunt Lottie's been a bad influence," I grumbled under my breath as I kissed the top of Grams' head in greeting.

Grams busted out laughing at that. "Don't go blaming anyone else, young man. She may only be seven, but she's brighter than you think, and perceptive. Maybe you should keep that in mind when your midnight romps are sneaking out of your place in the morning," Grams warned. "There may be acres between us all, but the fields are bare now, and her bedroom window is on the second floor."

"What's a midnight romp?" Lily looked up from her bowl at us.

I laughed, backing myself up toward the kitchen to dish up some chili. "Yeah, *Grams*, what's a midnight romp?"

Grams lobbed her napkin at me, cursing me under her breath as I darted out of the room cracking up. Served her right.

After finishing our dinner, we moved to the living room, where Lily and I played with Colton on the floor for a bit. Grams sat in her recliner, watching us as she sipped a cup of coffee, a soft smile worn on her face.

"Did you figure out who the mystery girl was?"

I flicked my eyes to her. "Yeah. No thanks to you."

She hid her sardonic grin behind her cup as she took another drink.

"And don't think I'm not onto you. And Lottie, for that matter." I pointed an accusing finger at her.

"I have no idea what you're going on about," she said, feigning ignorance.

"Yeah. Sure you don't. You should know better, Grams. Whatever you're scheming in that head of yours is not gonna work."

She huffed, setting her cup down on the end table. "Is it so terrible for a dying old lady to want to see her first grandson happy?"

I scoffed, shaking my head. "Now see, if you'd said your *favorite* grandson, we might be having a different conversation." I winked. "And you're not dying."

"I very well could be," she argued. "Besides, I don't tell lies. Tucker is my favorite." She pursed her lips, trying to contain her smile.

I ignored her challenge and her playful jab. We both

knew she was in perfect health. She'd probably outlive us all, at this rate. "You lied about knowing who Devin was—"

"I had no way of knowing she and the mystery girl were one and the same."

"And I *am* happy," I continued.

"Hmph," she grunted her disbelief, picking up her coffee again. "Well that poor girl obviously isn't. And it sounds like she could use a good man in her life. From what I heard, she had her heart broken."

I'd come to the same conclusion after meeting her that first night. Even though I knew I was playing right into Grams' hand, I still couldn't help but ask, "What are you talking about?"

"You hadn't heard?"

I narrowed my eyes at Grams. She'd already won this battle, there was no sense in her rubbing it in. She had me and she knew it. She glanced over at where Lily was blowing raspberries on her baby cousin's belly, making sure she wasn't paying any attention to our conversation.

"Apparently, she had a little outburst in Ida's yesterday morning. I won't go into detail, but sounded like she had a conversation on her phone that would've been better to have kept private." Grams raised an eyebrow.

I knew Grams wasn't judging. She was only looking out for Devin. She knew I'd likely want to do the same. Grams was one of the few people who knew about my past feelings for Jenna, and how I'd attempted to stop her wedding years ago.

"That's too bad." I looked back at my niece and nephew,

trying to pretend I wasn't bothered by the whole situation—the gossip about Devin, the fact that some asshole had hurt her. "Someone should probably warn her about how word spreads around here."

"Yes. *Someone* should."

"I'm sure Lottie and the girls will fill her in tonight," I said, hiding all emotion in my voice as I kissed Colton and Lily's heads before standing up. "Gotta go, kiddos."

"Where you headed off to?" Grams asked as I bent down, giving her a quick hug and peck on the cheek.

"Oh, you know..." I took a small step back. "Got a midnight romp waiting for me to pick her up."

Grams' hand shot out, barely missing my arm. I laughed, taking off before she managed to get out of her recliner and whack me good on the back of the head.

5

DEVIN

Wes had taken off once again, leaving me standing in a cloud of dust at the bottom of the steps. I wanted to get in my car and leave too, knowing they probably already thought I was a nutcase after the gossip going around town about my outburst in Ida's, and having found me crying in an alley the other day.

But I sucked it up, mainly because they already knew I'd arrived. When I'd looked up toward the house, I saw the curtains closing quickly as the girls tried to duck out of view.

Taking a deep inhale, I lugged myself up the porch steps and knocked on the door.

I was glad I hung in there. As soon as I knocked, they had immediately eased my worry, welcoming me into their fold without making me feel like an outsider. Conversation was easy and funny during dinner as I got to know Leighton, Lottie, and Hannah better.

I'd learned Billy and Leighton were siblings and Leighton had fallen for and married his best friend, Aaron. They had no kids and she wanted to wait a bit longer, since her job as a kindergarten teacher exposed her to plenty daily.

Lottie and Tucker were high-school sweethearts who rekindled their love over a decade later. They were now married, raising Tucker's niece, Lily, who'd lost her parents tragically, and their three-month-old son, Colton.

Hannah and Billy had initially been a one-night stand, but they fell in love and had recently married and were expecting their first child.

After hearing all their sweet love stories, I'd avoided discussing my recently failed relationship, guiding the conversation a different direction before they could ask. They didn't seem to notice, or were kind enough not to press me, most likely because they already had a good idea of what had happened.

We had since moved to the backyard to sit under a beautiful pergola lit up by string lights and a fire pit in the middle. The wood crackled as the fire burned, releasing a comforting smoky smell as we sipped on our wine, wrapped in blankets, laughing.

I hadn't been this relaxed in what felt like months. And I hadn't had this much fun in what sadly was probably years. Until now, I hadn't realized how badly I needed a night just like this.

"So, let me get this straight," Hannah said, her eyes still wide. "Not even once? You've never gone down on Aaron even one time? Not even on your honeymoon or for his birthday?"

"Hell, no. This dolly is a one-way trolley. I don't want that shit in my mouth." Leighton scrunched up her nose.

"I have no idea how Aaron puts up with you if you aren't constantly giving him head." Hannah sat back in utter dismay.

Lottie and I both erupted with laughter.

"Ha ha," Leighton mocked us all. "Trust me, my man has nothing to complain about."

"I'm with Leighton," I interjected, still giggling. The wine had completely disintegrated my nerves around these women. It was like I'd known them my whole life. I figured that was why I was having no qualms about sharing details of my sex life after just meeting them.

"You're telling me you've never given head either?" Hannah turned to me.

"Oh, no. I have...once. And it was terrible. He had whiskey dick, it was like a never-ending blow job."

They all looked at me, half-shocked and half-horrified.

"Whiskey dick is the worst. Anything longer than twenty minutes and you might as well start charging. What a terrible first, no wonder you're turned off." Hannah sighed, as if she truly felt sorry for me.

Lottie nodded her head in agreement as she took a sip of her wine. "So, you never tried it on anyone else?" Lottie asked.

I shook my head. "Nope. Not that I wouldn't...it's just...the last guy I was with wasn't circumcised. You never know what kind of cat is under that hat."

They all laughed. I grinned. It felt good to throw a jab at Noah, even if he wasn't present to take the hit.

"You know what we need right now?" Leighton spoke up. "A night out on the town. A true ladies' night!"

Lottie and Hannah both groaned. "Leighton. Seriously, give it up already."

Leighton ignored Lottie. "Plus, what better time than while we have a DD?" She pointed over at Hannah's overgrown belly.

Hannah responded with her middle finger in the air.

"The night *is* still young..." I said, and all three heads whipped my direction. I ducked lower in my chair.

"See!" Leighton cheered, rising to her feet. "That's what I'm talking about." She gave me an animated high five.

"Well, shit," Hannah sighed. "Fine. Let's do this. Might as well get in all the fun I can before this baby comes." She rubbed a hand over her belly.

"Do you mind if we stop at my place so I can change?" I asked, remembering the stares I got the last time I'd shown up at Dudley's.

"Oh no, lady," Lottie protested, helping a struggling Hannah to her feet. "We got you covered."

All three women had wide grins on their faces, and I got a sudden sinking feeling I'd just managed to sign myself up for something I hadn't intended to.

———

I TUGGED at the bottom hem of the black mini the girls had forced me into. I'd been struggling with the skin-tight dress the entire walk up to Dudley's front door, pulling at the bottom, only to have to tug at the top, so I wasn't revealing too much cleavage. We'd stopped at Lottie and Hannah's boutique on the way. They dressed me and did my makeup and hair like I was their personal Barbie doll.

I was just glad they allowed me to wear a pair of cowgirl boots like Leighton, versus the tall-ass heels Lottie wore. I didn't mind heels at the office, but once I was home, I preferred my Chucks or no shoes at all. When given the choice, I'd pick boots over heels every time. Especially these ones: they were black, with intricate tan stitching. I fell in love with them as soon as I saw them.

Lottie pulled open the door for us. Leighton led the way, followed by Hannah, then me. I tugged at the dress one more time as I passed through, and Lottie slapped at my hands.

"Cut that out, Devin. You look hot and you're gonna have everyone in here talking about the new girl in town."

"That's what I'm afraid of," I muttered, dropping my hands and straightening my back, my feet stalling at the threshold.

Lottie nudged me and I shuffled forward. She looped her arm through mine, full of confidence as she guided us through the bar to the table Leighton and Hannah had claimed.

I took a seat, already feeling like all eyes were on me and hushed whispers were circling around me. It was the first public appearance I'd made since my scene at Ida's. I had no idea now why I'd agreed this would be fun.

"I've got the first round of drinks," Leighton said, standing from her seat.

"What do you want, Devin?"

"Oh. Um. Whatever you guys are having."

"Easy enough," she said as she took off toward the bar, squeezing between the packed bodies. She was back quicker than I expected, with three bottles of beer and a glass of water for Hannah.

I took a big swallow, needing the buzz I'd been feeling earlier from the wine to return. We fell back into easy conversation, the same way we had earlier in the night. I had begun to relax and somewhere along the way, no longer cared if the town was talking about me behind my back.

"Lottie?" A small voice interrupted our conversation. We all turned to look at the blonde standing behind Lottie. I immediately recognized her from the first night I'd been here.

"Oh. Hey, Mandy," Lottie said with little enthusiasm and a plastered smile.

"Sorry to interrupt, I was just curious if you'd heard from or seen Wes tonight?"

"I'm his sister-in-law, Mandy. Not his keeper."

She forced her own smile onto her face as she glanced over at me and then back to Lottie. "Right. Well, it's just, we had a date tonight and he cancelled last minute. I just wanted to make sure he wasn't sick or something." She delivered her words almost as if she was bragging, rather than truly being concerned for him.

I shifted uncomfortably in my seat, unable to process how I felt about everything she'd just said. He'd really been headed for a date when I saw him earlier. Part of me thought he was only testing my reaction when he said that. Knowing that wasn't the case shouldn't bother me. But it did.

"Nope. He was perfectly well when I saw him a few hours ago," Lottie tossed out flippantly, turning her back to Mandy.

The girl looked like she was about to blow a gasket, and I almost felt sorry for her until she turned her eyes on me and they narrowed. She gave me a once-over and then, with a dismissive toss of her hair, she walked away. I had no idea what problem she could possibly have with me and frankly, I wasn't going to waste a second more wondering.

"This round is on me," I said, standing from my seat. "Who wants a tequila shot?"

All three hands went in the air.

"I'll have him dress you a shot of water, Han," I promised as I laughed and headed for the bar.

Timmy smiled as soon as I approached, making his way to me immediately. "Dr. Chaplin, what can I get ya tonight?"

"Call me Devin, Timmy."

"We're on a first-name basis, now? Does that mean you forgive me for calling Deputy Hill?"

"No. But I'll consider it as long as you keep the shots coming tonight."

He raised both eyebrows.

"Calm down, Timmy. I have a DD." I pointed my thumb

over my shoulder toward where Hannah sat. "I'll take three shots of tequila and one shot of water."

He chuckled, grabbing four shot glasses and lining them up to make our drinks.

"Thanks, Timmy, keep my tab open." I smiled at him as I picked up the drinks with both hands and headed back to our table.

As soon as I returned, the girls' conversation cut off awkwardly, their eyes refusing to meet mine.

"So, how about them Dallas Cowboys, huh?" Hannah threw out randomly as I set their drinks in front of them.

Lottie and Leighton both glared at her.

"Like that wasn't obvious," Leighton muttered, taking a drink from her beer.

Hannah shrugged. "Sorry, it's the first thing I could think of."

"Really? Because all of us sitting here are such big sports fanatics?" Leighton scolded.

"What's going on?" I asked, taking my seat as my stomach twisted into knots, suddenly worried I'd misjudged what I thought were going to be new life-long friendships.

"Will you two stop it." Lottie narrowed her eyes on both Leighton and Hannah in a silent warning before turning to look at me. "Sorry, Devin. I'm just going to be up front. We were talking about you."

"Ooookay..." I shifted in my seat uncomfortably.

"Nothing bad! I promise. It was more about the way Mandy acted, and the fact that she had the nerve to come over here."

"I'm confused. How does that have anything to do with me?"

"Isn't it obvious?" Leighton asked.

"Um...no?"

"She feels threatened. She's one of Wes'—shit." Lottie looked toward the other two for help. "How do I say this and not make him sound like a complete douchebag?"

Hannah snorted a laugh as Leighton piped up, "She's one of his regular booty-calls."

"Will someone cut her off, please?" Lottie snapped, pointing her glare at Leighton.

An uncontrollable laughter bubbled up and burst through my lips.

Maybe it was the alcohol, or the thought that Mandy assumed I was a threat to whatever she and Wes had, or that for some reason, the women I was sitting with seemed to agree. Either way, I was finding this all quite hysterical.

"It's fine, Lottie. You don't have to try and cover for Wes. There's nothing between us and there never will be."

All three ladies exchanged dubious looks. Admittedly, the words sounded like a lie even to my ears.

"Seriously. Besides, even if I thought he was cute, I'm not in a place to start a new relationship."

"Oh, Wes doesn't do relationships," Leighton announced as she lifted her shot glass to her lips.

"Seriously!" Lottie released an exasperated sigh as she swiped the shot glass from Leighton's hand and took it herself.

Leighton stared at her in utter shock, then reached for

Lottie's tequila. But Lottie was too quick and downed that one too.

Hannah cracked up laughing, and I couldn't help joining in with her as the two childhood best friends had a stare off. It only lasted seconds before they both busted out giggling, too.

"Are you sure about you and Wes?" Lottie tried again once the laughter died down. "Because things seemed pretty tense between you two outside my house earlier."

I bit at my lip. It was harder to deny how being around Wes made me feel when my guard was weakened with alcohol. "I'm sure. Like I said, I'm in no place. I'm sure you girls probably already know that after what happened the other day."

They all three nodded, looking at me with understanding expressions. "You don't have to talk about it. We won't pry," Hannah offered, and the other two nodded in agreement.

"Honestly...I kind of do feel like talking about it. I mean why the hell not? Right? Everyone already knows the worst of it, that the man I thought I'd be spending the rest of my life with was fucking his co-worker on the side for months and I didn't have a clue. Not until I walked in on them of course... I mean, then I had more than a clue. I had her tiny white ass in my face."

"Asshole," Leighton chimed in, stealing Hannah's shot of water. She emptied it, then slammed the glass on the table. Spinning to face the bar, she did some sort of weird baseball signal aimed at Timmy across the room. The only thing I could figure was she was trying to order us another round.

"How long were you guys together?" Hannah asked.

"Four years. Four freaking years I wasted my life on him. Which is exactly why Wes and I will never happen. I made the mistake of falling for a playboy once, I won't do it again." I took my shot. "No offense, Lottie," I added before biting into my lime.

She put up both her hands. "None taken. I know his reputation as well as anyone. But I also know he's a good man with a big heart behind that wall he's built to guard himself. I just have no idea why he's chosen to hide it."

Her admission surprised me, but I didn't have a chance to think about it long before Leighton was putting her two cents in once again.

"Well, don't sweat it girl. You have the right idea. I don't know why women always gotta be jumping into that shit. There's a reason there are toys for the tidbits."

"You've been married longer than all of us. I don't know what you're preaching on about," Hannah commented.

"Exactly." She lifted her finger in the air, as if she'd made a profound proclamation. "I have the most valuable input here. Play the field, girl"—she pointed her finger at me —"and don't tie yourself down too fast. Not that I regret it... There's a reason I locked Aaron down when I did."

Timmy chose that moment to show up with another round of shots for us. "Ain't that right, Timmy?" Leighton slurred.

Timmy placed the shot glasses on the table and snatched up the empties. "Anything that comes out of your mouth,

Leighton, is either a load of bull shit or a load of horse shit."
He smirked with his adorable eyes.

She smacked at his arm and he flinched away, chuckling. "You got these ladies under control?" he asked, looking over at Hannah.

"What do you think?" She grinned.

"That's what I was afraid of," he sighed, walking away.

6

WES

"What's up man?" I asked, answering my phone as I headed out for a night with Mandy.

"Your old man just called the station. Sounds like some high-school kids are out on your land again. I was about to get off duty. You want me to handle it?" Roger asked.

I opened my truck door, glancing across the dark, open fields, where I could hear the faint sound of music echoing from Tucker and Lottie's place. The whole house was lit up, and I could smell a fire burning in the distance. Just thinking about Devin sitting around that fire, with the women I considered to be family, had me tugging on the bill of my hat. I knew I should get as far away from here as possible, before I changed my mind about this hook up.

Damn it.

"Yeah. I'll meet you out there. They in the same spot as usual?"

"Yep, down at the river," Roger confirmed. "I'm about five minutes out."

"Okay. I'll see you there." I ended the call and then shot Mandy a text, letting her know I wasn't going to make it, all while I tried to convince myself it had nothing to do with Devin.

I'd already been second-guessing whether I should go out with Mandy. I'd started to get the feeling she was wanting more from me than just the occasional fuck. She was one of the only girls I messed around with on the regular, mostly because she was fun and didn't seem to care what I did. But lately, it seemed she was taking that to mean more than it did.

It'd probably be best if I ended things with her altogether before she got hurt. But I wasn't going to do that over a text. I wasn't that big of an asshole. It was a conversation I needed to have with her in person.

When I saw a pair of high beams light up the pitch-black sky, I shook my head with a smile. I guess the girls called it an early night and were heading home. I gave one final look at Tucker's place as I crawled into my truck.

———

ROLLING to a stop next to Roger's squad car, I took in the scene in front of me. Four kids stood by the tailgate of an old

Chevy truck, looking scared shitless as his car's spotlight shone brightly on them.

Roger exited his car, meeting me at the side of my truck. "You recognize them?" he asked in a hushed voice.

"I recognize one of them. That's Ricky Logan. He's the starting quarter back for varsity this year, isn't he?"

"Yep. And the other boy is his star receiver."

"Well, this should be fun," I said in a low voice, being sure to wipe the grin off my face before we walked where they could see.

Roger took the lead, shining his flashlight in Ricky's eyes as we got closer. "You kids wanna tell me what you're doing out here on private property?"

"Nothing, sir," Ricky spoke up first, stepping away from his friend and the two girls they had with them as he shielded his eyes with his arm. "Just hanging out, that's all."

"We didn't know it was private property," one of the girls bravely added. The other one looked like she was near tears.

"Uh, huh," Roger said as I crossed my arms, doing my best to keep a straight face and look pissed. "You may not have, but these boys did. Ain't that right, Zack?" Roger aimed his flashlight to the right, now blinding the receiver.

The boy's posture stiffened with a new wave of fear. "We didn't mean any harm by it, Deputy Hill."

Ricky stepped back toward the braver girl, putting his arm around her. "We just wanted to find a good spot to look at the stars, sir."

I choked on a laugh, using my fist to cover my mouth and fake a cough. These boys were full of shit. Roger turned to look at me over his shoulder, giving me a warning look so I didn't blow it. As he did, Zack slyly slid his foot to the side, kicking something under the truck tire. But he wasn't sly enough. Roger saw it at the same time I did and pointed the beam of his flashlight to the spot where an empty beer can peeked out from behind the rear tire.

"What do we have here?" Roger asked as he walked closer to the truck, shining his light inside the cab.

He opened the door and looked around and under the seat, pulling out a poorly hidden twelve pack of Miller Light. He walked back to the rear tailgate, where the second girl was seriously about to cry, her friend with an arm around her trying to calm her.

"It's not ours!" Zack said in a hurry, and Ricky smacked him. "Ouch." Zack rubbed at his shoulder.

"Not yours, huh? Funny...I think you boys told me that the last time. Interestingly enough, there's never anyone else around to claim it."

"Aww come on, Deputy Hill, can't you cut us a break? You know what it's like growing up in this town. There ain't shit to do," Ricky pleaded.

"So, you think underage drinking and trespassing on private property is the answer?"

All four kids shook their heads. I had no idea how Roger kept a straight face while lecturing them. We had done the same damn thing growing up, with exception of the trespassing, since my family owned most the land surrounding town.

"Does your coach know you boys are out here drinking during football season?"

They shook their heads and Roger looked toward the girls. "What about you two? Your parents know?"

"No, sir," the braver one answered while the other one whimpered.

Roger let out a heavy sigh as he turned his back to them, smiling and winking at me as he walked toward me with the partially full box of Miller Light. His smile vanished as he turned back around, his face hard and tone stern.

"I'll tell you what. I'm gonna let you off with a warning this time for the drinking. But if I catch you kids again, I'll be calling all your parents. *And* your coach... I'll have to confiscate this beer, though. As far as the trespassing, I'll leave that up to Mr. Monroe, since it's his property."

All four pairs of eyes flicked to me as they waited for my verdict. I shook my head in feigned disappointment, dropping my hands to my hips, maintaining a firm look on Ricky. "How much you had to drink?" I asked. There was no way I was letting these kids drive off on their own if he'd had too much to drink.

"Barely finished half a beer, sir, when you guys drove up."

I could see in his eyes he was telling the truth. "All right, then. Get these girls home now, before I change my mind."

"Yes, sir," he said as they all moved quickly to climb into the truck.

"Oh, and Ricky..." I hollered.

"Sir?" He stopped, looking back at me just before he climbed into the driver's seat.

"Good game last week."

"Thanks, sir," he said, both of us grinning ear to ear. He

shut his door, turning over the ignition, wasting no more time getting the hell out of there.

As their taillights disappeared down the road, Roger held up the half-empty box of beer with a wide-ass smile. "I'm officially off duty. You got time for a beer?"

"They cold?"

"Mostly."

"Good enough for me," I said with a friendly slap on his back as we walked to my truck, popping the tailgate.

———

"*Damn...Jenna* Hamilton...now there's a blast from the past. *Jenna...Jen-na.*"

"Will you quit saying her name like that?"

"Like what?"

"All slow and shit. And repeatedly. Just stop saying her damn name."

We'd been shooting the shit all night on my tailgate when he'd brought up Devin. It seemed I couldn't go anywhere without her being a topic of conversation. Roger had only been giving me a hard time about me owing him double now after the ride home he'd given her and the beer he'd inadvertently provided us when she initially came up.

"I'm sorry, man. I'm processing here. This is some funny shit, Jenna and that doctor being cousins..." Roger chuckled silently beside me as he took a drink.

"It's not funny."

"It's funny to me."

"You're a dick. I don't know why we're friends."

"Because who else could you get to drive drunk chicks home and steal you free beer from high-school kids?"

"You got a point." I grinned, taking down the last swallow of my beer. I tossed the empty can into the back of my truck bed and grabbed another.

"And who would've guessed?"

"You should've," I scolded. "You should've fucking known the night you took her home and warned me, so I didn't get blindsided."

He shrugged. "I didn't ask for her family tree, just her address." He tossed his own empty and grabbed the last beer, popping the top open.

The sound of the beer cracking open and fizzing filled the gap in our conversation. We both sipped on our beers, listening to my radio play in the background.

"So, what are you gonna do?" Roger broke the lull.

"Nothing."

I felt his eyes on me as I stared straight ahead at the river.

"Really?"

"Yeah. Really."

"All right, man," he said with a single shake of his head, lifting the can to his lips. "We're out. You wanna head to Dudley's after this?"

And that right there is truly why we were friends. Because unlike most people in my life, Roger knew better than to push me.

"Why the hell not," I agreed, downing the last of my beer.

———

ROGER LED the way to the bar after we stopped by his place for him to change out of his uniform and into civilian clothes. It wasn't often he got a Friday night off, so he was always down for a night out when he had the chance.

We entered through the rear delivery door, shaking Timmy's hand on our way through the backbar. The three of us had all gone to school together and grown close over the years. Timmy hadn't run with Roger and me back in the day. He'd been more into the music scene than the sports we played.

"What's happening, Timbo?" Roger asked, helping himself to a beer in the under-counter cooler.

Timmy picked up his rag, resuming his efforts in drying off a few glasses to mix up some new drinks. "Getting my ass kicked, that's what," Timmy grumbled.

The man worked every day of the week, refusing to hire a manager to give himself a night off. He didn't trust anyone to run things the way he liked. Couldn't blame the man. Dudley's was his baby. And it was the best joint in town because of his hard work.

He passed the freshly made drinks off to one of his waitresses before grabbing three shot glasses. "Your women are gonna drain me of all my tequila, Monroe."

"My women?" I asked, turning my eyes where he'd jerked his chin toward.

Even if he hadn't pointed me in their direction, my attention would have been drawn to the rowdy table of women surrounded by men cheering them on as they took back-to-back shots of tequila, then chugged a beer.

Roger walked up beside me, where I stood fisting the beer he'd handed me, watching as Leighton and Devin raced to the finish. Devin beat Leighton by half a beer, slamming her empty onto the table, immediately throwing her hands in the air as she screamed in victory. Leighton flipped her off. Lottie and Hannah laughed. Then some jackass picked Devin up, spinning her around in some sort of celebratory dance.

I scrubbed a palm over my mouth as I controlled the possessive impulse coursing through my veins after watching the dipshit with his hands all over her. And what the fuck was she wearing? She hadn't been wearing that when I saw her earlier. The tight dress rode up, nearly exposing her ass as he lifted her higher in the air. My fist clenched as I nearly lost my shit.

Roger gripped my shoulder, pointing the neck of his beer bottle toward the table. "Yep. Probably best you do nothing. I don't think even you could handle a woman like that."

"Someone should probably warn Bradley he's gonna have his hands full tonight," Timmy said, joining us as we watched the wild scene unfold.

"Why the hell are you still serving them?" I growled at Timmy.

"They have a DD. And you try cutting them off. I already tried twice and nearly got my ass kicked by Leighton and Dr. Chaplin. Besides, this is your fault," he said, pointing a finger at my chest.

"How the fuck is this my fault?" I asked, peering over at Timmy.

"Because the doc made me promise to keep the drinks coming to make it up to her for calling Roger the other night."

"Still not seeing how any of this shit is my fault," I argued, staring back over at the table, where the guys were now trying to convince Lottie to let Leighton take a shot from her stomach.

For fuck's sake. What is this? Girls Gone Wild?

"Tucker is gonna kick all of our asses if we don't get this shit under control." I pointed to where they were all now chanting Lottie's name. Thank God she was refusing, but I wasn't sure how much longer she'd hold out before they convinced her to do it.

7

DEVIN

I clutched my stomach, laughing while everyone continued to chant Lottie's name. My abs ached from all the laughter tonight. I felt alive. I hadn't acted this wild and crazy since college. And though I knew I'd probably have some regrets in the morning, it felt so damn freeing to just let loose.

Lottie laughed as she kept shaking her head adamantly. She'd stopped drinking nearly an hour ago, letting Leighton and I battle off.

"Okay, boys!" Hannah hollered over the ruckus. "I don't think you're gonna get her to accept this challenge."

I had no idea when the guys had joined us. But at some point in the night, they'd parked themselves at our table, throwing different drinking challenges at us. If we completed it, they paid for a round of our drinks and vice versa.

They were here for a bachelor party. They'd driven over

from another town not far from here, looking for a good time for their buddy. The soon-to-be groom was now passed out drunk in their car in the parking lot.

The chanting died with Hannah's announcement, and was replaced by good-hearted booing and groans. Most of the guys dispersed, headed for the bar, except for the one who'd been flirting with me all night.

"How about we get out of here?" Ben asked, whispering into my ear with his arm draped across the back of my chair.

Releasing a small laugh, I tucked my head to the side, lifting my shoulder to my ear where his voice had tickled it. He was cute and maybe in another lifetime I might have said yes. But before I could say anything, a large figure suddenly loomed over my back, silencing the whole table.

"How about you get lost?" an authoritative voice demanded.

I didn't need to look to know who'd just issued that threat.

Ben stood taller as he looked from me to Wes. "Excuse me?"

"You heard me."

"Look man, no disrespect, but I'm talking to Devin here."

"Well, she's not interested," Wes stated sharply.

"I think *she* can speak for herself," I finally snapped, coming out of whatever state of shock I'd been in, and spun to glare at Wes.

His face was hard as he glared right back at me with a clenched jaw and a frown line across his forehead. My heart thrummed anxiously against my ribcage as we silently stared each other down. All eyes were on us, volleying between Wes, me, and Ben like they were watching a tennis match.

Ben finally broke the silence. "You said you were single." He took a step back.

"I am," I grated between my teeth, still glaring at Wes.

"Well whatever this is, I'm not getting in the middle. Maybe another time, Devin," he said, picking up his beer and walking away.

I tore my eyes from Wes to watch Ben's retreating back. I hadn't changed my mind. I had no plans on going home with him, but I was still livid that Wes felt he had the right to speak for me.

"What the hell was that?" I spun on Wes, my blood boiling, ready to pummel him.

"I'm gonna get another round!" Leighton chirped hurriedly.

"I'll go with you!" Lottie volunteered, jumping from her seat.

"I gotta pee!" Hannah threw out as she eased herself from her seat as quickly as she could.

I'd barely registered a word they said as all three of them rushed off, leaving me alone with Wes. "I can't believe you just did that!" I yelled.

He roughed a hand through his hair, glancing away from me to where Ben now stood at the bar with all his buddies. "Were you seriously going to go home with that guy?" he growled, throwing his arm out from his side in Ben's direction.

"No!" I blurted, my chest heaving.

The stiffness slowly faded from his shoulders as he registered my admission, the wrinkles in his forehead softening and smoothing. And for some reason, the rage I'd been feeling started to dissolve.

"But even if I was," I added in a much calmer voice, trying desperately to make my point anyway, "it'd be none of your damn business."

A slow smile tipped his lips as his eyes pierced mine. "Dance with me."

"What?" My eyes grew with the fluttering in my tummy. "No!"

"Come on, Doc." He nudged me playfully. "Dance with me."

"I said no."

"Doc." His smile widened.

"No. And what is wrong with you, anyway? You can't just show up here, scare away the only guy interested in me, then expect me to dance with you."

"He's not the only guy. If you think that, then you're not as smart as I thought."

"Oh? And who else in here is interested?"

"Every man in here is interested. They're just intimidated."

"By you?"

"No. By *you*."

"And you aren't?"

"I'm not trying to get in your pants right now. I'm just trying to dance with you."

My head cocked with a raised eyebrow at his "right now"

clarifier. He continued to smile that intoxicating smile. And I tried my best to hold on to some of the anger from earlier, but the man was making it nearly impossible, weakening whatever defenses I had left.

"Come on, brown eyes. I promise to keep it PG." He winked.

I rolled my eyes. "If I dance with you, will that shut you up?"

"It's worth a shot."

He held out his hand for me as Chris Stapleton's "Tennessee Whiskey" began to play. I took it, following him to the dance floor. Tugging at my hands, he pulled me close, and I linked my hands at his neck, closing my eyes, resting my cheek on his chest. My whole body warmed in his arms as a wave of tingles trickled through me.

I concentrated on steadying my breathing and reminding myself nothing could ever happen between us, no matter how badly my body was begging for him to touch me everywhere. With our bodies pressed so tightly together, swaying to the seductive beat of the song, I was afraid I'd lose that internal struggle.

"You're awfully quiet. What's up, Doc?" he prodded, his head dipping so his lips brushed against the crown of my head, sending shivers down my spine. His voice was full of a knowing cockiness.

I opened my eyes, glancing down between us, where I felt his hard-on pressing against me. "Apparently, you," I quipped, looking up at him with an equally cocky smile.

His head fell back. His gorgeous green eyes crinkled at

the corners with his loud laughter as he peered back down at me. "Can't blame a man. Especially when you're wearing that dress." His eyes fell to my chest before looking back at my face.

"What's wrong with my dress?"

"Not a damn thing," he whispered, gliding the tips of his fingers over my cheek, and tucking a few strands of hair behind my ear. His other hand increased its pressure against the small of my back, forcing us closer together.

Staring up at him, my whole body heated. My heart raced, sending vibrating tingles to every limb. The urge to taste his lips was suddenly winning over my morals. His head lowered and I closed my eyes again as he poised our mouths inches apart.

All it would take was for me to lift slightly onto my toes. Our lips would press together. And the anticipation, the curiosity, would all end. I felt myself giving in, his warm breath sucking me in, his whole body dragging me under a wave of lust. I rose slightly and a throat beside us cleared.

I jumped, pulling back, breaking out of his arms abruptly as we both looked over to the person who had interrupted us.

Mandy stood there, a saccharine smile on her face. "Mind if I cut in?"

"Mandy—" Wes started, his face and tone firm.

"Of course," I said, taking another step back as I got my wits about me. "He's all yours." I spun to leave.

Wes latched onto my wrist. "Devin."

"It's fine, slick... Besides, you two had a date tonight, isn't that right?" I glanced at Mandy with a forced smile and then back at Wes. "I'm sure that's why you're here."

His face pinched in confusion, his grip loosening. I twisted my wrist from his grasp and took off, pushing through the crowd to find the girls. They were back at our table, and from the expressions on their faces, they'd seen everything. They stood instantly, grabbing our things to leave. It was in that moment, I knew these girls had my back, and that knowledge alone made me want to burst into tears. Lottie's arm was around my shoulders immediately, ushering me out the door as the other two followed behind us like a shield of armor.

———

I GROANED as I rolled over, silencing my phone. *Noah. Again.* I crawled out of bed, tripping on the boots I'd worn last night and stubbing my toe on the dresser.

Mother. Effer.

I hopped on one foot, stumbling into the bathroom with nothing but my panties and a tank top on in search of some headache medicine. Twisting off the cap, I popped two Excedrin into my mouth and washed them down with a handful of cold water from the faucet.

Looking at my reflection in the mirror, it didn't take long for all the regrets from the night's events to hit me like a sledgehammer. Wes Monroe and our almost-kiss being at the top of the list. *No more tequila. Ever. Again.*

I splashed some water on my face, brushed my teeth, and

pulled my hair up into a knot on top of my head before walking back to my room to tug on a pair of jeans. I cuffed the bottom hem of each pant leg. There was a drafty chill in the air, causing me to rub at my arms as I searched for a flannel button down in my closet. I slipped my arms through the sleeves, leaving it open, exposing the tank top I still wore underneath, and headed to the kitchen in need of some coffee.

I leaned against the counter as I waited for it to finish brewing, mentally comparing my outdated kitchen to Lottie's beautifully renovated one. When I bought my house, it was in decent shape and exactly what I wanted: an older home in an established neighborhood, original wood floors, two bedrooms, one bath, and a nice front porch where I could sit and drink my morning coffee.

I knew there would be things I wanted to update, like the kitchen and bath, in the future. For the most part, all the house needed was a fresh coat of paint throughout and maybe some new landscaping, which I planned to do myself in the coming spring. But all the updates would have to wait. I'd decided getting settled into my new life and job was my primary focus.

For now, the house was perfect. And mine. Only mine. Knowing that was both empowering and slightly depressing at the same time.

I blocked the latter part of that thought, reaching for a mug to fill with the freshly brewed coffee. I grabbed a yogurt from the fridge and made my way to the front porch for a quick breakfast. I sipped from my mug on the porch swing, with my bare feet resting on the seat's edge as I texted Leighton to see if she and Aaron could give me a ride to the Davis farm later. After leaving Dudley's last night, Hannah had dropped us both at our houses in town before driving Lottie and herself home.

Once she had confirmed, I set the phone aside and enjoyed my coffee, nursing my hangover while soaking in the peacefulness of my neighborhood. With the final sip, I stood from the swing. It was time to get to work on unpacking the last of the moving boxes in my house.

————

BOBBING my head lightly and swaying my hips a little to the sounds of Fitz and The Tantrums' "Handclap" blasting through my house, I hung my last family photo on the wall in the hall that led to the bedrooms and bathroom. It was one of my favorite pictures of Jenna and me from her wedding. As I stepped back to admire the photo collage I'd hung, there was a knock on my front door.

I padded toward it, carrying the hammer I'd been using. There was another knock, this time delivered with the catchy rhythm of "Shave and a Haircut." A small grin graced my face. Leighton was obviously not letting a hangover bring down her mood. She'd been much worse off than me last night, so I could only imagine hers was ten times more painful. Or maybe she bounced back easier than me.

I swung open the door, a giant smile on my face that slipped instantly. "What are *you* doing here?"

"Come on now, brown eyes. Is that any way to greet a man who came all this way to do you a favor?"

I crossed my arms over my chest, my defenses going up. "What favor?"

"I figured you might need a ride to the farm, seeing how your car is still parked there."

"Well it's a shame you came all this way, because I have a ride already," I hissed, slamming the door in Wes' face.

My tense shoulders relaxed as I walked away to finish decorating my living room. My steps stalled with more pounding on the door behind me. Ignoring it, I pushed forward. As the pounding increased, I increased the volume of my speakers, hoping he'd get the hint and go away. Forever.

8

Her music blared through the screens of her open windows. I chuckled at her attempts to ignore me. If she thought I was going away that fucking easy, she was in for a surprise. There was no way I was leaving her front porch until she had that cute little ass firmly planted in the seat of my truck.

I took a wild guess and fired off a text to Aaron, letting him know I'd be giving her a ride to the farm and not to worry about it. He responded a few seconds later with the numbers "10-4."

I slipped my phone back in my pocket, stepping to the side to look through her living room window. I couldn't help the wide-ass smile on my face as I watched her dance around, placing trinkets and books on some bookshelves.

I stepped back, inspecting the edges of the screen before popping it out of the window frame and setting it to the side.

Lifting a leg, I crawled through her window and into her house while her back was to me. She bent over, reaching into the box in front of her.

My dick twitched, seeing her in that position. It'd already been growing against my pants from watching her shake her damn hips to the rhythm of the music. Without thinking, my hands flew to those taunting hips, gripping them tight.

She screamed, jumping as she spun, kneeing me in the balls.

Fuuuuckkkk. I groaned, folding over as my hands instinctively cupped my dick.

"Oh my God!" she screeched, her hands flying to her mouth. "I'm so sorry!"

"What the hell, Doc?" I half-growled half-groaned, still hunched over.

She scurried across the room to turn down the music. Taking a few deep breaths, I stood upright to look at her, the pain still radiating as I moved my hands to my hips.

Whatever remorse she initially might've felt was gone. She mirrored my stance as she glared at me. "What the hell are you doing in my house?"

"You wouldn't answer the door."

"So, you resorted to breaking and entering?"

"You didn't really leave me a choice."

"You're absurd," she scoffed, walking toward her front door, flinging it open. "Get out," she demanded.

"If you kick me out and force me to leave, how do you expect to get your car?"

"I already told you. I have a ride."

"You mean with the Bradleys? Yeah. They're not coming."

"How did you—" She stopped herself, her eyes squeezing shut as she took a deep, calming breath. Her eyes flicked open and narrowed. "I don't believe you. You're lying." She flipped a hand toward the opened door, silently directing me to leave.

"I wouldn't lie."

"You broke into my house," she pointed out, her tone still full of accusation.

"You're right. You should probably call the cops."

"I would, but they're probably all your drinking buddies and it'd do me no good." She gave me a sarcastic smile.

I dug into the front pocket of my jeans, pulling out my phone and navigating to my text exchange with Aaron. Walking to stand directly in front of her, I lifted my phone to her face, so she could read it.

Her eyes widened as they roamed across the screen. "Oh my gosh. You're certifiably crazy."

I lowered the phone with a proud smirk, tucking it back away. "Told ya."

Her eyes thinned again. "It doesn't matter. I'll find another ride. I'll call my aunt and uncle."

"You're really going to call them and interrupt their Saturday morning when I'm standing right here, offering to take you?"

"Yes."

Pivoting on my heels, I walked away and took a seat on her couch, stretching my arms across the back of it, exaggerating the process of getting comfortable in her home with a loud sigh.

"What do you think you're doing?"

"Waiting for you to get your shoes on."

"I said I wasn't going with you."

"And I'm telling *you*, I'm not leaving here until you do."

"You're annoying," she huffed.

"I prefer persistent. And most women like it. It's part of my charm, I've been told." I winked, giving her my smile that had those same women dropping their panties within seconds.

"Well, I'm not most women," she argued.

I had no doubt about that. It's the exact reason I figured I couldn't get her out of my mind, no matter how hard I tried, or how bad of an idea I knew it was to pursue any kind of relationship with her.

After our dance last night and having been so close to kissing her, knowing she wanted me to, I was done fighting the inevitable. I wanted Devin Chaplin. And I was going to fucking have her. Maybe if we screwed and got it out of our systems, I could move on with my life and get back to not caring what she was doing every minute of every day.

I didn't respond to the very true statement she'd just made. Instead, I leaned forward, reaching for her remote.

"You're serious," she gawked.

"As a heart attack," I retorted, flipping on her TV and settling back against the couch, suppressing a smile.

Five. Four. Three. Two—

"Fine."

Arching an eyebrow, I looked over at her agitated expression.

"If it's the only way to get you to leave, I'll let you take me to my car." She slipped on a pair of flip-flops that sat in her entryway. "But if you give me one of your smug grins or stupid winks, I'll slap that smile right off your face," she warned.

I contained my grin as best I could, standing to meet her at the door. I wanted to do more than just take her to the farm. I wanted to take her to my bed. Baby steps, though. I may have decided to give in to my urges, but it was obvious Dr. Chaplin was determined to keep up the charade.

"You sure you don't want some boots or something? The temperature is supposed to keep dropping today."

"I'll be fine," she insisted, waiting for me to lead the way.

My lips twitched with another grin, knowing it was highly likely she'd slam the door and lock it behind me as soon as I stepped across the threshold. "After you," I taunted.

She huffed, grumbling something inaudible as she stomped from window to window, closing them. Snatching her purse and phone from the entry table, she walked straight out the door. I flipped the lock on the knob, shutting the door as she continued her tantrum on the way to my truck.

She flung open the passenger door and I broke into a light jog, not missing the opportunity to put my hands on her again and help her into my truck. Her body stilled for a beat with my touch. Taking a deep inhale, she continued to climb onto the seat. My grin was huge behind her back, knowing she'd felt *it*. The same way I had. I was even more confident she wouldn't be able to fight against that feeling much longer.

After closing her door, I ran around and hopped into my truck, glancing over at her profile as I put the keys in the ignition. She continued to ignore me, scooting herself against the passenger door. Amused by her hardheadedness, I shook my head, turning over the ignition. Slinging my arm over the back of her seat, I looked over my shoulder as I reversed out of the driveway.

She peered from the corner of her eye at the bag of fresh pastries sitting on the console between us, the sweet aroma filling the cab. I'd stopped to pick them up on the way to her house, along with two coffees.

"There's a cinnamon roll in there with your name on it."

"You got me a cinnamon roll?" Her expression twisted with surprise as she lifted her eyes from the bag to me.

I shrugged it off like it wasn't a big deal. When I'd stopped by Lottie's earlier this morning, she might have thrown me a bone that Devin had been obsessing over them the night before.

I'd seen Devin's car parked outside her house during my early rounds on the farm. It didn't take Lottie long to figure me out. She knew I'd shown up unexpectedly to see if Devin had stayed over, not because I was hoping Tucker was already home, as I claimed. He was due back today, but we both knew he wasn't arriving until this afternoon.

Devin bit at the corner of her bottom lip as she stared at me from across the truck. "Why would you do that?"

"Figured you might be hungry. Lottie said you liked them. It's not a big deal, Devin. Really. Just eat it already."

She reached for the bag, pulling out the cinnamon roll.

"Mind handing me the muffin?" I asked.

"Sure," she agreed, pulling out my favorite breakfast muffin from Ida's—maple pecan—and passing it to me.

Taking the first bite of her cinnamon roll, she hummed in appreciation, and my dick rose in appreciation. I shifted in my seat, adjusting myself discreetly. We both ate as I drove us through town, turning right at the courthouse, taking the highway that led out of town.

"Where are you going?" she asked, covering her mouth as she spoke through her last bite of the cinnamon roll. "This is the wrong way," she mumbled, and then swallowed.

"Didn't I mention I have a small errand to run first?"

I felt her eyes burning holes in my profile as I continued to stare out the windshield. We both knew damn well I never said a word about my errand. And to be honest, I hadn't meant to bring her along with me, but now that I had her in my truck, I wasn't in any hurry to let her get out of it. Plus, having a vet with me for this particular errand wouldn't hurt.

"Wes," she reprimanded.

"Doc," I mocked.

"This isn't funny. I have plans. Take me to my car. *Now*."

"What plans?" I asked, my muscles stiffening, wondering if she had a date planned with the jackass from last night.

"I need to finish unpacking my house."

I relaxed only slightly with her response, a self-inflicted

tension still lingering in my body. I shouldn't care if she had a date, I reminded myself.

"That can wait. And no sense in arguing. You might as well relax and enjoy the road trip."

"Your list of criminal offenses is growing. First breaking and entering, now kidnapping."

I laughed, glancing to the side. Her tone had been full of amusement. She tucked her lips between her teeth, holding back a smile.

"What can I say, you bring out the worst in me." I leaned on the middle console with my right elbow as I steered the truck with my left hand. Her sweet perfume flooded my nose at our closeness.

She scoffed a laugh. "Oh, now it's my fault?"

"All I'm saying is, I've had a clean record up until you showed up."

"I doubt that. You probably just never got caught, or were given a free pass because you're *you*."

"What's that supposed to mean?"

She sighed, shaking her head. "Nothing... Where are you taking me, anyway?"

"Dillon."

"Dillon! Wes, that's almost four hours from here!"

"Nice to know you're familiar with your Texas geography, Doc."

She squinted her eyes at me as she kept up the ruse of being angry, even though it seemed she was anything but.

"So, you kidnap me and take me to one of the smallest towns ever to exist."

"Less witnesses that way."

She rolled her eyes, slipping off her flips-flops, resting her pretty little toes on the dashboard. "What's in Dillon?" she asked, picking up the coffee I'd bought for her and taking a sip.

"A horse. There's a man just outside of Dillon who has a filly for sale. We've been looking for a horse, so Lily can have one of her own. Tucker sent me a message this morning asking if I could drive over there to check her out."

"That's nice of you."

I lifted my left shoulder in a shrug. "It's not a big deal. I know he's anxious to get home to his family today. Besides, it's a gift from both of us, so no reason I shouldn't go instead of him. If it works out, we plan to give it to her for Christmas."

"That's sweet."

"What?"

"Just that you guys would do that for her."

"You think she'll like it?"

"What little girl wouldn't want her own horse for Christmas?"

"Yeah, I guess you're right."

I snuck another look at her as she focused her attention on the road ahead of us, seeming more relaxed than she'd been when I first showed up on her doorstep, but still struggling to just let loose. We rode in silence as the music played on the radio. Chris Stapleton's voice began to croon through the speakers, singing the song we'd danced to the night before.

She stiffened as a blush crept across her cheeks and then groaned, playing off her uncomfortableness as she reached for the dial. "Does anyone listen to anything other than country music around here?"

"Like what? That music you were listening to back at your house?"

"Well, yeah. Exactly," she said, turning it to a local alternative station.

Her toes—still on the dash—started to tap in sync with the beat, drawing my eyes to them. How could anyone's feet be so damn sexy?

I cleared my throat, needing to get something off my chest, needing to clear the big-ass elephant the last song had inconveniently conjured. "I'm sorry about last night... For Mandy..."

She looked out the passenger window, hiding her expression from me. "It's fine, Wes. What you do or *who* you do, is none of my business."

From any other woman I was hoping to sleep with, the words from her mouth would've been music to my ears. But from her, it felt like a slap to the face. And I didn't like to think about why that might be.

"Either way, I didn't like how our dance ended."

"I'm sure things turned out just fine for you at the end," she commented under her breath.

"Hey." I reached over, squeezing just above her knee.

Her eyes lingered on my hand that remained on her leg before she raised them to my face.

"I didn't sleep with Mandy last night," I stated simply, my eyes flicking back and forth between her and the road.

I wanted her to know the truth.

She didn't respond verbally. She let her body do all the talking, dropping her feet to the floorboard and shifting her knees away from me, so I'd be forced to remove my hand.

I wanted to insist on keeping it there, but it was obvious she needed whatever space she could get in the confines of my truck. I pulled back, shifting my own body away and placing both hands on the wheel, tightening my grasp as I clenched my teeth. Putting more space between us was the last thing I wanted to do, but if it was what she needed, I'd respect that.

———

Parking the truck outside a roadside diner, I opened my door without saying a word. When she didn't make a move, I looked over at Devin. We'd both been silent for the last couple hours as we drove, listening to music. I allowed her to continue to control the radio. It was the only peace offering I could make that she'd willingly accept. I'd caught as many glimpses of her as I could on the drive without steering us into a ditch, but she hadn't returned a single one of them. She'd been lost in her head the whole ride.

"Are you coming?" I nodded my head toward the diner. "Figured we could use a break from the truck. Grab a bite to eat for lunch."

She nodded, attempting a half-smile, unbuckling her seatbelt.

I itched to touch her as we walked toward the entrance. As soon as the moment presented itself, I brushed her lower back with my fingers as I opened the door for her, guiding her inside first. That slightest touch triggered the strongest need I'd ever felt for a woman.

I smiled at the hostess, raising two fingers. She seated us immediately in a booth by the window. We looked over the menu without a single word uttered between us, only speaking to give our orders to the waitress.

The uncomfortable silence that persisted was driving me nuts as I stared at Devin sitting directly across from me. Physically, she was mere feet from me, her knees mere inches. But mentally, she was miles away. She fiddled with the straw wrapper in front of her, tearing it into tiny pieces, concentrating on it like it was the most important task in the world.

When she could no longer shred the paper any further, she glanced up, her eyes locking with mine. The throb in my chest increased.

She was fucking beautiful.

She had no idea.

Her phone vibrated on the table in front of her, drawing both of our eyes to the screen. I barely caught the name of a guy before she was hitting ignore and turning her phone face down. Her expression flipped like a switch, going from somber contemplation to irritation.

That same possessiveness I'd felt the other night simmered below the surface. The feeling scared the hell out of me. I'd never felt it before for any of the women I'd been with, much less for one who could barely stand to be in my presence the way Devin seemed she couldn't.

She turned her head to stare out the window, drawing herself back into the seat, her hands falling to her lap under the table. She was pulling farther away from me, making me only more desperate for her attention, her voice.

"You've got beautiful eyes," I stated, telling her exactly what I'd been thinking.

With a hard swallow, her eyes fell shut. Her chest heaved as she took a deep breath.

"I don't even mind that the left one's lazy," I added with a teasing smile, hoping to ease the tension my compliment was obviously causing. The last thing I wanted to do was cause her more turmoil.

A throaty laughter erupted from her mouth as she looked back at me, her head shaking slightly as she did.

I grinned, winking at her, relieved it worked.

"I do *not* have a lazy eye," she argued with a smile.

"Maybe not. But it's nice to see you laugh... Every time I see you, you look sad. Or pissed."

She casted her eyes downward as she sighed. "I guess I'm not great at this 'starting over' thing..."

"Not sure I follow."

From where I was sitting, she was doing just fine. She'd already managed to get my sister-in-law, Hannah, and Leighton on her side. I had to grovel just to get any information out of Lottie this morning. If she gained their respect and protectiveness already, she'd have no problem finding her place here.

She shrugged, her shoulders curling inward as her hands lifted to fidget with the straw in her water. She remained quiet for a few beats, stirring it around, creating a mini tornado inside her glass.

"It's like I've been sleepwalking through life," she finally spoke, "trying to be this person expected of me for the last four years and somewhere along the way I lost myself. I'm finally waking up and I have no idea how I ended up here or where to go from here."

"Does this have anything to do with that phone call the whole town is talking about?"

She turned her head back to the window without answering me.

"I'm sorry," I immediately apologized, knowing it was none of my fucking business. But I couldn't help my curiosity.

I wanted to know every damn thing I could about this woman. I wanted to protect her from whatever asshole had made her upset, and was still making her doubt herself. It was a complete contradiction to the strong, confident woman I'd witnessed over the past week.

Leaning forward, I started to reach for her hand that sat idle on the table, but was interrupted by the waitress bringing our food. I eased back, dropping my hands under the table, annoyed by the interruption.

"Two burgers, all the way," the waitress announced,

setting our plates in front of us. "Can I get you two anything else?"

"No. Thank you," I replied quickly, hoping she'd leave as suddenly as she appeared.

Devin gave the waitress a small smile in agreement. There was a beat of awkward silence as our server walked away.

"I need to say something about our conversation in the truck earlier," Devin fiddled with the napkin in her lap before meeting my eyes.

I picked up my burger, nodding my chin for her to continue. I didn't have a good feeling about whatever it was she was about to say.

"I'm the one who should've been apologizing, not you. My life is a mess at the moment. And I shouldn't have let things...*progress* the way I did. I can use all the friends I can get right now, so the last thing I want to do is ruin a potential friendship."

"There's that word again...*friends*," I grumbled as I picked up my tea, taking a drink.

"You say it like it's a bad thing." She reached for a fry on her plate, dipping it in the side of ranch dressing she'd ordered.

I set my glass down, pinning her with my eyes. "What if I told you I'm not sure I can be your friend?"

"I don't know..." she admitted nervously, her hand halting. "Is that what you're telling me?"

Shit. Was I? What if she told me it's all I could have with her? The thought wasn't a pleasant one. It's not what I wanted. Maybe she was right to insist on it, though.

We were on dangerous ground, and as much as I wanted to risk it, wanted her to fall into my bed, there was no guarantee that one time would be enough for me. Enough to get Devin Chaplin off my damn mind. And the last thing I wanted was to dig myself into a deeper hole.

I wasn't a one-woman man. Pursuing things with Devin might push me into a corner I didn't want to be in. I was already having stronger feelings for her than I was prepared for. She was a heartache waiting to happen.

"No, brown eyes. If friends is what you want, that's what we'll be."

She dropped her eyes to her plate, a partial smile on her lips as she resumed dipping her fry. "Thank you." She popped it into her mouth, seeming relieved.

———

AFTER OUR LUNCH, the atmosphere of the truck had been the opposite of the first half of the drive. Devin was fun as hell when she let loose. She was schooling me on all her music as we compared the playlists on our phones. While mine was full of country music, hers was full of alternative bands.

I actually liked some of what she had and planned to download the songs later. Specifically, the one currently vibrating through my truck, which she informed me was "Electric Love" by the Borns. But I wasn't about to admit that out loud, because I loved how fired up and passionate she got about the songs when I'd scrunch my nose at her selections, pretending to hate them.

Eventually, we agreed to disagree on who had the best music, moving on to other topics. Most of them were about our families and our lives growing up.

"When the sheriff showed up, I thought your uncle was gonna kill me," I said, smiling as I got lost in the memory. "She went wild child, riding in the bed of my truck. She was screaming, her arms spread wide, like she was Rose on the Titanic. I was too busy watching her in my mirrors going crazy as hell to worry about anything else." I laughed, thinking about one of the best times I'd had with her cousin, Jenna.

I wasn't sure how Cricket had come up. Maybe because both our childhood memories involved her.

She laughed with me. "Sounds like you brought out a different side of Jen."

"Yeah, guess so," I agreed, my laughter slowly dying as I remembered the way Jenna and I were together.

"Did you love her?"

My eyes flicked to Devin, caught off guard by her question. I cleared my throat as I looked back at the road. "Of course. She was one of my best friends."

"That's not what I meant," she pressed, and for the first time, I had my answer on how much Devin might know about our could've-been relationship.

I frowned as I considered her question. "I thought at one time, maybe I could love her as more than just a friend...but I don't know that I was ever truly in love with her. We never took that step for me to really know," I admitted. The last thing I wanted to do was lie to Devin.

The way she continued to study me made me feel like I was under a microscope. "She's happy. I think it's important you know that. She's very happy with two beautiful little girls. You did the right thing that day."

"What are you talking about?" I played dumb. I knew exactly what she was talking about. The moment she was referencing.

"I don't know that I should be telling you this, it's not my place or my business," she sighed as she struggled with an internal debate. "I know what happened the day of her wedding. I know she went looking for you. I know what she told you and what you told her. She's my best friend, Wes. We tell each other everything... You broke her heart that day, but you also freed her heart, so she could love her husband fully."

I shifted in my seat uncomfortably. I didn't want to talk about Jenna anymore. Not because I was harboring old feelings, but because I was more interested in the woman sitting next to me.

9

DEVIN

"Have you ever had your own horse?" Wes asked, immediately changing the subject.

I didn't push to discuss his history with Jenna any further, figuring it might still be a sore subject for him. But I meant every word I'd told him. He'd made the right choice for her, and part of me hoped it'd been the right one for him, too.

"Sadly, no. I've lived in the city my whole life. Growing up in a condo in downtown Austin doesn't exactly allow for having a pet horse."

"That *is* sad. Especially knowing they're your favorite... What about now?"

"Ha!" I scoffed, jokingly. "Not sure my half-acre lot in the middle of town is the best place for one either."

"You can always keep it at my place. We have plenty of room."

"I appreciate the offer, but I couldn't ask that of you."

"You didn't. I offered," he pointed out. "And what are friends for, if not to give you free stabling for your horse? My bed is also open, if *you* ever need a place to stay. As friends, of course," he teased.

"Wes," I warned, playfully narrowing my eyes at him.

Every time he smiled at me with that wide grin, I felt my heart rate pick up. I ignored the thudding in my chest and shook my head in amusement, cranking up Judah & the Lion's "Suit and Jacket," desperate to drown out the voice in my head saying maybe I'd been hasty to suggest we only be friends.

Wes turned off the highway onto a small country road. Within minutes of the turn, we were slowing to a stop outside an old white barn that needed a fresh coat of paint.

After slipping my feet back into my flip-flops, I opened the door and slid from the seat. The chill in the air nipped at my toes, and I hated to admit I should've listened to Wes about putting on a different pair of shoes. In my defense, I had no idea he'd be taking me for a joyride across the state at the time. It had very little to do with my being stubborn and rebellious.

Wes met me at the side of the truck, taking my hand in his as he walked beside me to the pens, where a beautiful American quarter horse was being held.

"Is that her?" I asked, trying my best to ignore how natural and perfect it felt for him to hold my hand the way he was.

I should remove it.

Put some acceptable space between us.

Blurring the lines of our friendship was only going to make things more difficult for me. I was having a hard-enough time putting aside my growing feelings for the man. A man I knew was only physically available.

Wes released my hand as we neared the metal pipe fence. I gripped the top rail, stepping up on the bottom rail so I could get a better look at her. Wes smirked as he looked over at me. Even with the boost, he still towered over me. I gave him a warning look as he opened his mouth, knowing a wise-crack about my height was on the tip of his tongue.

"Wes Monroe?" a deep, gruff voice asked.

We both looked behind us at the stocky, balding guy striding our way. His protruding belly and chest heaved; he looked winded from the walk he'd just made. I glanced around, wondering where he'd come from to be that sweaty and worn out.

"Yes, sir," Wes replied, shaking the man's hand. "Thanks again for letting me come see her today."

"No problem. Just hope you didn't waste a trip. Billingsley is a long way from here."

"That it is, but so far so good." Wes looked back over at the prospective filly. "She looks like a healthy horse."

I followed his gaze, watching her strut in circles around her pen. She was a beautiful rich brown with a shiny black mane. Her only markings were black stockings on all four legs. Lily was going to love her.

"How's her temperament?" Wes asked, reclaiming his previous spot beside me at the fence.

"She's as calm as they come. She'll be great for your niece. She may be young, but she's trained and been broke in plenty. Ridden by my own grandkids," the old man said, sidling up to the fence on the other side of Wes.

"What do ya think, Doc?" Wes asked, nudging my shoulder with his as he rested one boot on the bottom rail.

"She's gorgeous. Mind if I take a closer look?" I asked the man.

"Clark Thomas, meet Dr. Devin Chaplin," Wes said, adding a late introduction.

Clark's eyes widened slightly, as if he was just noticing me for the first time. "Pleasure to meet you, Dr. Chaplin." He offered me a pudgy hand. I shook it and then discreetly wiped the dampness he'd left on my palm down the side of my jeans. "And of course. Have at it." He jutted his chin toward the horse.

I jumped down from my spot as he opened the gate. I was immediately chiding myself again for not putting on a pair of boots. Wes followed me inside the pen, allowing me to take the lead in inspecting the horse up close.

She'd definitely been broken in. There was no hesitance on her part. She immediately strode toward us, nudging and sniffing at our hands.

"She's looking for carrots," Clark chuckled from the fence line. "Afraid that's my grandkids' doing. Now she expects anyone coming to visit her will have some for her."

I smiled, running my hand over her neck. "Sorry, girl. No carrots today."

I continued to pet her before moving my hand to the

mandibular artery, just under her jaw. I took her heart rate, making sure there were no signs of a murmur. I gave her as thorough a checkup as I could without my kit.

Wes kept her calm, brushing his hand alongside her neck as I worked.

"Well, what's the final verdict, Doc?" he asked.

"She's healthy. In great shape. Perfect really, as far as I can tell."

Wes smiled at me before turning his head. "Looks like you got yourself a deal, Clark," he hollered.

"Well, hot damn!" Clark fired back, slapping his knee with a loud smack.

The two men shook hands in agreement before Wes was saddling her up to take her for a short ride in the open field.

While Wes rode her, I hung out with Clark at another pen, where his men worked with a beautiful, black stallion.

"What's wrong with him?" I asked as I watched the horse rear up on his back legs, kicking his front hooves outward in agitation. He grunted and snarled like he was ready to charge the trainers.

"He's been running hot since the day he got here."

"Is he sick? He seems irritable."

He chuckled. "There's nothing wrong with this one physically. He's just strong-willed and stubborn as hell. Not a fan of being roped or penned up."

Sounded like another stallion I knew, except he had an aversion to being pinned down rather than penned up. I glanced over my shoulder in the direction Wes had disappeared to take his new horse for a run in the field.

Clark sighed as his trainers continued to struggle. "This one here may be untamable."

The thought pained me more than it should. It had little to do with the horse in front of me, and more to do with the sexy man now striding toward me. I'd known it from the start. Getting close to Wes Monroe would only end in heartbreak.

———

"Safe and sound. As promised," Wes said, shifting his truck into park next to my car.

The expansive sky was painted black, with stars shining brightly overhead. I didn't make a move. Wes had the heater blasting on my toes. The temperature had dropped to the low forties and I was in no hurry to leave the comfort of his truck and step out into the cold air. And secretly, I wasn't quite ready for our road trip to end.

"Thanks for coming with me, Doc."

"You didn't exactly give me a choice," I taunted.

"Well, in that case, thanks for not kneeing me in the balls again."

I laughed and he grinned at me, giving me one of his damn winks. I wasn't sure if I found them more charming or annoying at this point. The man was growing on me.

"No problem," I replied as my laughter died. "Thanks for the ride."

"Anytime, sweetheart," his warm voice whispered.

His eyes heated as they held mine. Every inch of my body

burned, and it had little to do with the hot air coming from the truck's vents. If I didn't force myself to leave immediately, I knew things would end up going a direction I wasn't ready for again. And I wouldn't have the alcohol to blame this time.

"I should go," I breathed.

"Your choice."

His words were a challenge. Friends or more... He was leaving it up to me.

I gripped the handle, pulling on it to open the door before I had second thoughts. Planting my feet on the ground—literally and figuratively—I looked back at him. "Later, slick."

"Night, brown eyes."

His grin was the last thing I saw as I closed the door, hurrying to jump into my car. I blasted the heater the whole way home, with a never-ending smile on my own face.

————

LEANING BACK IN MY CHAIR, I bit at the end of my pen as I stared at my cell phone lying face up on my desk. It was opened to my list of contacts, frozen on a very specific contact. One that started with a 'W' and ended with a 'Monroe.'

I'd not so slyly gotten his number from Hannah the other day when I stopped in their store to see her and Lottie. I tried to play it off, giving them what seemed like a legitimate reason why I needed it. They both just exchanged a knowing look.

In hindsight, saying I needed it so he could give me a recommendation on the best place to buy boots *was* obvious. Especially considering who I was talking to in the moment and where I was standing.

But shamefully, I'd become desperate. It'd been almost two weeks since our impromptu road trip. I hadn't seen or heard from Wes since then. Though I knew it was probably for the best, I couldn't help the disappointment I felt every day that went by with no sign of him.

It was silly of me. There was no reason for him to call or stop by to see me. We'd agreed to be friends, nothing more. Plus, he'd basically put the ball in my court when I left him that night in his truck.

I tossed the pen on my desk, sitting forward to pick up my phone. This was stupid. I should just call him. Friends called each other all the time.

There was a knock on my office door. Tina cracked it open, popping her head in. "Hey, I'm headed to lunch. Want me to bring you anything back?"

It'd become part of her daily routine lately, since I'd been choosing to work through most of my lunch breaks. I felt a little guilty, but she assured me it was no problem.

"Oh. Um." I glanced back at the phone in my hand, my thumb hovering over the call button. I lowered the phone and stood from my desk. "Do you mind if I come with you?"

"Really?" The pitch of her voice went an octave higher as her eyes went wide as saucers.

"Yeah. I mean, if you don't mind?"

She smiled. "Of course not! I'm just a little surprised is all. I'd love it if you came. How do you feel about Kathy's?"

"Sounds good to me," I said, picking up my purse and slipping my phone inside.

———

I FOLLOWED behind Tina as we walked inside the bustling diner. The aroma of fried foods, the boisterous chatter, the clinking of silverware against plates, and the clanking sounds from the kitchen all surrounded me. I immediately relaxed into the atmosphere, fond memories rushing back to me.

I hadn't been to Kathy's since I was a young girl. It was a frequent stop for us during the summers I spent here. Uncle Robert would bring Jenna and me here for a treat. We'd gorge on burgers, fries, and chocolate milkshakes. From what I remembered, it was the best comfort food I'd ever had. And that was saying a lot, considering I'd grown up in Austin with some of the finest restaurants.

Tina and I sat at one of the few open booths near the front, snatching up the menus that were propped between the salt and pepper shakers on the table.

I perused the menu, settling on the club sandwich and fries. A few minutes later, an older woman appeared at the side of our table.

"Afternoon, ladies," she smiled.

"Hey, Miss Debbie," Tina responded, lowering her menu. "Have you met Dr. Devin Chaplin?"

"I haven't had the pleasure. But I've heard enough about

her. Nice to meet you, Dr. Chaplin." Her eyes twinkled with mischief.

I blushed. Unfortunately, after my outburst in Ida's, my reputation had continued to precede me. "Nice to meet you, Miss Debbie."

With a single nod of acknowledgement, she pulled out the pencil tucked behind her ear. "Are you two ready to order?"

We both nodded in response before giving our orders. Tina and I chatted as we waited for our food. She was great company, and I hadn't realized what little effort I'd made to get to know her since starting work.

I admitted that to her and apologized for not doing so. She brushed it off and told me she understood I was just busy settling in. But I made a promise that from then on, I'd make it a point to get to know her and our vet techs better.

We were halfway through our lunch when I felt eyes on me. I lifted my head, searching the room. A heated tingle swarmed my body as I watched Wes' confident stride coming toward me.

"Doc. How ya been?" he asked, stopping next to our table.

I cleared my throat. "Good. I was thinking about calling you," I anxiously blurted.

"Is that so?" He smiled.

I swallowed another lump in my throat and nodded. "Yep."

Resting his hands on the table, he leaned in, putting his face inches from mine. "Well, maybe next time you shouldn't just *think* about doing it," he suggested in a low voice. His lips twitched as he held back his smile, standing upright once again. "Later, Doc." Looking across from me, he tipped the bill of his hat. "Tina."

"Wes," she murmured his name with a breathy sigh. Both of our eyes were glued to him as he walked out of the diner with a couple guys I didn't recognize. "Oh, what I'd give to have him look at *me* that way," she said, fanning herself.

I looked back at her in shock. "Tina!"

"What?" she asked, unashamed. "I'm not the only one. I think every woman in this town would sell their soul to tie that one down. He's the full package. Sexy. Charming. Wealthy. Loves his family. Whatever woman manages to rope him is one lucky bitch."

I scoffed. "I'm pretty sure that man has no intention of settling down."

She lifted an un-dissuaded shoulder. "I think he just hasn't met the one, yet."

Or maybe he has. Maybe he just let her go and now he was set on being single forever. The thought of Jenna and him extinguished whatever thoughts I was starting to have about Wes and me. The same way it did every time.

———

RESTING my forehead on the tips of my fingers, I massaged my temples. After lunch, we returned to the office and I felt a headache slowly growing with intensity throughout the afternoon. I lifted my head in search of some medicine in my purse, determined to stick it out until the end of the day.

The office phone rang and seconds later, Tina stood in the opening to my office. "It was Noah, again."

"Ugh," I groaned. "I'm so sorry, Tina. If you need to threaten his life, feel free to do so."

I'd blocked Noah's number and since then he had resorted to harassing me on my work phone. Unfortunately, his harassment started and ended with Tina. Another reason I told myself to make it a point to be much nicer to the woman. She was a saint for screening his calls for me.

She giggled, leaning into the frame. "I may just do that."

I laughed with her and another sharp pain shot across the back of my head. "Shit," I cursed under my breath, clutching my head.

"Everything all right?"

"Yeah," I lied, then cringed with another sharp pain. "Actually, no." I released a defeated sigh. "I think I'm gonna head home for the day. My head is killing me."

"Still?"

"Yeah."

"Then you should definitely go. Don't worry about your last appointment. I'll let Dr. Hamilton know. If he can't cover, I'll reschedule."

"Thank you, Tina. Has anyone ever told you, you're the best?"

"Only every day." I could hear the humor in her voice.

I grinned through the pain. "Well, I'm telling you again."

———

I CHANGED into a pair of sweats and one of my favorite concert tees, completing the outfit with a pair of fluffy gray socks before curling up onto my couch with a blanket and hot cup of tea.

I felt like crap.

I was just glad it was Friday evening. If this turned out to be more than a migraine, at least I wouldn't miss too much work, having the weekend to heal and recover.

As I settled back, getting comfortable for the night, ready to watch a marathon of Netflix shows until I passed out, there was a knock at my front door, startling me.

I glanced at the clock, confused. It wasn't extremely late, but definitely too late for unexpected visitors. If Aunt Jane hadn't called earlier to check on me, I would've assumed it was her.

Placing my cup on the coffee table, I flipped my blanket to the side and stood to answer the door. I peeked through the peephole and jerked back, shocked by who I saw standing on my front porch. My eyes dropped to my clothes, my hand flying to my hair that was a mess on top of my head.

I chided myself silently, lowering my hand to my side. There was no reason to care what I looked like. Determined to stick to my guns, I flicked the lock on the door. If I was lucky, he'd take one look at me and run for the hills. I twisted the knob, opening the door to where he stood, looking sexy as ever with his cap twisted backward on his head and a grocery bag in his hand.

10

I pounded on the door, waiting impatiently. It finally creaked halfway open, revealing Devin on the other side.

"Hey." The word was faint on her lips.

My eyes did a slow crawl down her body as I checked for any sign of what might be wrong with her. "How do you feel?"

"Just peachy," she shot from her smart mouth.

I tilted my head to the side with a furrowed brow. Stepping forward, I lifted my one free hand to her forehead. I'd barely made contact before she was slapping it away.

"What are you doing?"

"Checking to see if you have a fever."

"Do I look that terrible?" she asked, crossing her arms defensively over her stomach.

"You couldn't look bad if you tried, brown eyes. I heard you were sick."

"How is that even possible?"

"Word travels fast 'round here. You should probably keep that in mind before trusting anyone with your secrets."

"And who do you trust?"

"No one."

"Of course," she huffed. "Well, thanks for your concern, but I'm fine."

"Your aunt says otherwise. I ran into her at the grocery store. She might've mentioned you went home sick from work today."

"Well, she shouldn't have. It's not a big deal."

I ignored her, reaching for her forehead one more time.

She slapped at my hand once again. "Will you stop that!"

"This is my fault. I shouldn't have let you leave the house without real shoes."

She looked exhausted as she sighed, resting her head against the doorframe. "That was weeks ago. There's no way this is related. And even if it was, it wouldn't be your fault. It's just a migraine."

"You get those often?"

"No. Only when I'm stressed."

"What are you stressing about?"

"Nothing."

"Keeping that secret to yourself?" I taunted.

"Just taking your advice," she droned, her eyes dropping to my side. "What's in the bag?"

"Provisions. I got the one thing you need for anything

that ails you..." I grinned, lifting the bag with the Tupper-ware container. "Homemade chicken noodle soup. It should do the trick."

"You made me chicken noodle soup?" An emotion flashed across her face and was gone before I could identify it.

"No, Grams did. I just made the phone call and the trip to her house to pick it up. But hopefully that still counts for something."

She gave me an amused smile as she opened the door wider, stepping aside. I passed her the bag and she carried it into the kitchen around the corner. I slipped off my jacket, hanging it on the coat rack she had in the entry while my eyes scanned the cozy living room.

The couch sat centered in the room, anchored by two end tables with lamps, directly across from a large-screen TV mounted above the fireplace. White built-in shelves and cabinets flanked each side of the fireplace, already jam-packed with her things. Her place seemed like she'd been living here for years rather than weeks, with the way every room was already decorated and organized.

I walked over to the fireplace, where she had a couple of unlit logs stacked inside. Squatting down, I surveyed the handful of used matches piled off to the side. Shaking my head in amusement, I picked up the nearly empty box.

"You got an old newspaper or something?" I hollered over my shoulder toward the kitchen, where I could hear her tinkering around.

"Do people still read those things?" she yelled back.

I chuckled.

"Kidding! Check on top of the coffee table."

I glanced over at the table, finding last Sunday's local paper. I restacked the logs, pulling a few off to give the fire some room to breathe, then checked to make sure the damper was open. Crumpling up a few pages, I stuffed them under and between the logs. I lit the edge of a piece of the sports section, using it to ignite the rest of the paper. Within minutes the logs were starting to catch.

"You come all this way to light my fire?" she asked from behind me.

"I wish," I muttered, lifting from my knees.

"What's that?" She cocked her head, innocently.

"Nothing." I grinned over at where she stood just inside the living room with two mugs filled with soup.

"I made you one." She offered the one in her right hand, passing it off to me with a spoon.

"I brought that for you."

"I can share. She made enough for the whole town."

"You've obviously never had Grams' cooking, or you wouldn't be complaining about the amount, and you definitely wouldn't be so willing to share."

Giving me a soft smile, she took a seat on one end of the couch, pulling her feet onto the cushions and her knees to her chest. "Then I can't wait to try it." She cupped the mug with one hand as she lifted the spoon to her mouth.

I waited patiently for her reaction and within seconds of her first bite, she was humming with appreciation.

"Oh. My. Gosh," she mumbled through another bite.

"Told ya," I said proudly, taking a seat on the other end of her couch.

"Does she make the noodles from scratch or something?"

"Family secret," I responded, taking a bite myself.

"So, you don't know," she concluded.

"Hell no! That woman will probably take all her recipes to the grave. I'm pretty sure she even leaves off a few key ingredients in the church fundraiser recipe book," I grumbled.

She flung her head back with a hearty laugh. "Oh my gosh. You sound so bitter."

I grinned over at her. Every time I heard her laugh, it made my world a little brighter. Especially when I knew it was me making her do it. A deep-seated desire inside me wanted to make it my life's mission to make her laugh at least once a day.

"Were you about to watch a movie?" I jutted my chin toward the TV that was frozen on some introductory credits.

"Netflix marathon." She took another bite and then sipped some of the broth from her cup.

I sat my mug on the table, picking up the remote to hit play, then settled back into the couch.

"What are you doing?"

"It's getting late. We should probably get started."

"You're staying?"

"Unless you don't want me to." I glanced over at her, raising a brow.

"No. I mean, yes. I do. It's just...it's Friday night."

"And?"

"This is really how you want to spend your Friday night?" she asked, setting her mug aside to face me.

"It's exactly how I want to spend my Friday night." I reached for her ankles, pulling her fuzzy-socked feet into my lap, before looking back at the TV.

"Wes." There was a warning in her tone, laced with hesitation.

"Relax, Doc. The show's starting," I demanded, keeping my eyes on the screen. It wasn't until I felt her body do just that, that I glanced at her again.

"Before I forget to tell you," she yawned, her head nuzzling into a throw pillow. "Thank you for the soup. And the fire," she added sleepily as I began to gently rub at the soles of her feet with my thumbs.

"No problem, brown eyes. Now be quiet."

She nudged my stomach with her toes and I chuckled.

————

I WOKE up to something vibrating my leg. I rubbed at the crick in my neck as I lifted my head from the back of the couch. I glanced down at my lap where Devin's feet still rested, one sock now missing and the other making its way off her foot. The buzzing started again. Shifting as carefully as possible, I dug my phone out of my front pocket.

A missed call and a couple text alerts from Billy were on my screen. After looking at the clock on my phone, I rubbed a palm against the rough stubble on my face. It was four in the morning.

Fuck.

I was late for work.

I glanced over at Devin, who was still sound asleep. Lifting her feet as gently as possible, I slid out from under her. The last thing I wanted to do was leave her. I'd prefer to be carrying her to bed and curling up beside her for the rest of the morning.

Picking up the edge of her blanket, I adjusted it so she was completely covered. I flipped off the TV, setting the remote on the table. She moved and I stilled as she rolled to her side on the couch, mumbling something incoherent. When she settled, I instinctively leaned down, kissing the top of her head, taking one more good look at the softness in her expression as she slept. My phone started to vibrate again, and I swore under my breath as I sneaked out her front door, locking it behind me.

"Chill, Miller. I'm on my way," I barked, answering my phone on her front porch.

"You fucking better be. Your old man is pissed and taking it out on the rest of us," he grumbled.

"Shit. Sorry, man," I apologized as I rushed down the steps and to my truck. I jumped in and started it up. "I must have dozed off while watching a show."

"Where are you, anyway? And don't tell me at home because I already checked there. It's not like you to do an all-nighter at some chick's house when we have an early start. You with Mandy or something?"

"Hell, no. I ended that weeks ago. And not that it's any of your business, but Devin's."

"Devin. Huh."

"It wasn't like that, so keep your mouth shut. Or my dad won't be the only one kicking your ass today."

He laughed. "All right, man. Just hurry the hell up."

"Be there in ten," I confirmed before hanging up the phone and hauling ass past the city-limit sign.

———

"You boys get enough to eat?" Grams asked as she took a seat next to me at the table with Colton in her lap. His tiny fingers went for the butter knife and fork, but she pushed them out of his reach.

"Yes ma'am," Billy answered, nodding his head as he dragged his napkin over his mouth.

"Delicious as always, Grams," I added, standing from her table and kissing her cheek before picking up my dirty plate to take to the sink. Billy followed behind me with his own plate.

"Rushing off already? I have some fresh peach cobbler in there that needs to be eaten."

"Wish we could, but Dad's already in a piss-poor mood. We need to get back to work."

"And whose fault is that?" Billy muttered beside me and then grunted, glaring over at me as he rubbed the spot where I'd just elbowed him in warning.

Grams didn't miss a thing, the wrinkles in her brow deepening as she stared at us. The old woman was as sharp as a tack.

"Later, Grams. Thanks for lunch." I smiled, moving quickly to leave. Billy's steps were right on my heels.

"Now hold on just one minute," Grams commanded.

We both halted, glancing back over our shoulders.

"Billy, you and Hannah will be over for Sunday dinner tomorrow night." It wasn't so much a question as an order.

"Yes, ma'am," Billy agreed like a good little boy.

Pussy. I smirked.

"Wes, make sure to invite Devin over, too."

The grin on my face disappeared faster than shit off a shovel. "We're just friends, Grams," I insisted, not sure I sounded as convincing as I hoped.

"All the more reason. It's about time I met the girl in person. I've heard enough about her. Time to put a face to the name."

I nodded. No use in arguing. If I didn't invite her myself, Grams would figure out a way to get her there on her own. Might as well prepare Devin ahead of time.

Billy snickered beside me as we walked out of the house. I shoved him and he laughed harder, stumbling down the steps.

"Friends my ass," he cackled.

"Watch it, Miller. Just because you're married to City with a kid on the way, doesn't mean I won't still beat your ass."

He threw his palms up in surrender, making a poor effort at containing his now silent laughter. "Just find it hard to believe is all."

"What's so hard to believe?"

"You being friends with Devin. Unless... Oh, shit"—his

smile widened with his eyes—"she friend zoned you, didn't she?"

I ignored him, yanking open my truck door.

He climbed into the passenger seat across from me, still staring at me in shock. "She had to. Because there's no fucking way being friends was your idea. Either that or you're losing your touch, brother."

"I'm not your brother. I'm your boss. Remember that."

I backed the truck up, flipping it around and taking off down the dirt road toward the field we'd been working. Finally quieting, Billy rested an elbow on the edge of the open window as the cool autumn air rushed through the cab.

I glanced over at him, his words bugging the hell out of me. "How do you know I wasn't the one who wanted to be friends?"

His head tilted to the side. A silent stare of skepticism was his only response.

I focused back on the road. "Screw you. Mind your own business," I ordered.

He chuckled under his breath, annoying me more. Mostly because, maybe he was on to something.

Maybe I was losing my touch with the ladies. I'd been going through an abnormal dry spell. Since the first night I'd met Devin, to be exact.

My knuckles flexed as I fisted the steering wheel tighter. It was time to shit or get off the pot, I decided.

Billy jumped out of the truck as soon as I parked. He glanced back at me when I didn't make the same move.

"Right behind you," I said.

With a smug smile I wanted to punch off his face, he strutted off to fire up a tractor. I pulled out my phone, scrolling through my contacts.

Wes: How ya feeling?

I didn't have to wonder long whether she'd respond. The gray dots appeared immediately at the bottom of my screen.

Devin: Better. I think you were right about the soup.

Wes: Usually am. ;)

Devin: <eye roll emoji>

Wes: Glad you're feeling better. You got plans tomorrow night?

Devin: Depends...why?

Wes: You've been summoned for Sunday dinner.

Devin: Who's cooking?

Wes: Grams.

Devin: In that case, I'm wide open.

My grin widened. My fingers moved swiftly.

11

DEVIN

Another text-message alert dinged. Setting the spoon on the counter, I turned the stove down to a simmer before picking up my phone again. I bit down on the smile growing on my lips as I read the message.

Wes: Killing me, Doc. I'm getting visuals over here.

Devin: Mind out of the gutter, slick. FRIENDS.

Wes: You still set on that?

I started to type "no" as a knee-jerk reaction, then deleted it, my chest tightening. It was getting harder to deny the chemistry between us. Every little thing he did made it so easy to want to throw every doubt I had out the window.

Devin: What time tomorrow?

I held my breath, waiting for his response to my avoidance. I didn't want to lie to him, but I wasn't sure I could take that leap with him either. A change in subject felt like the best solution.

When a good two minutes went by with no reply, I sagged against the counter. I set my phone down and went back to making my lunch with a heaviness in my stomach. I was dishing up a bowl of leftover soup by the time my phone finally chimed again.

Wes: Six. I'll pick you up.

Devin: I can drive myself.

I was pushing my luck. At this point, he may un-invite me altogether. But that would be better than it feeling like a date.

Wes: Six, Doc. Be ready.

I set my phone down, only half-relieved. He didn't hate me. But I was pretty sure his patience was running out. I wasn't dumb enough to think he was good with being friends. I'd known the minute he agreed in the diner that it wasn't what he really wanted. It was written all over his face.

Problem was, I wasn't sure I was strong enough to take what he'd be offering: a good time in his bed with no strings attached. That wasn't me. That wasn't what I wanted. But part of me wondered if it was just what I needed. Jumping into a new relationship after barely coming out of a failed one was never a good idea.

————

I GROANED, tossing another outfit to my floor as I trudged back over to my nearly empty closet in my bra and panties. Over half of my wardrobe was scattered across my bedroom floor. I had nothing to wear.

No. Really. Nothing.

At least nothing that made me feel sexy, but not too slutty for Sunday dinner with his family, but still hot enough to impress Wes, without giving him the wrong impression.

Was that so much to ask?

I glanced at the clock on my nightstand. He'd be here in less than thirty minutes. I flopped backward onto my bed with a groan and stared at the ceiling, only lifting to my elbows when my phone began to ring. Jenna's name and smiling face flashed onto the screen and a wave of guilt flashed through me.

"Hey. What's going on?" I answered, sitting on the edge of my bed.

"Not much, just making brownies for the kids' fall fundraiser tomorrow. Mom said you were sick the other night. You okay?"

"Yeah. It was just a migraine."

"That sucks. But glad it wasn't something worse. What are you up to?"

"Uh, not much...just trying to find something to wear to dinner."

"Hot date?" she teased. The hopeful glee in her voice didn't help the rolling guilt in my stomach.

"Not exactly..." I let out a heavy breath, knowing I'd only feel worse if I didn't come clean. "I'm having Sunday dinner at the Monroes'."

The line fell silent and I pulled the phone from my ear, wondering if we'd gotten disconnected.

"As in Grams' Sunday dinner?"

"Yeah..." I chewed on my thumbnail.

More silence followed.

We hadn't talked much about Wes since her wedding, other than her informing me that he'd disappeared from her life altogether. His choice, not hers. She'd tried multiple times to reach out to him since, and every time her calls and texts went unanswered. She'd given up after six months of trying to no avail.

"Jen?"

"Yeah...I'm here."

"You okay? Is *that* okay?"

"What? Of course. I'm just shocked is all. Not that I should be. It's just...how is he?"

"He's good." Neither one of us needed to say his name. There was only one Monroe she'd ever be that concerned about. "He's single." I smacked my forehead with an open palm as I shook my head. There was no need to point that out.

She snorted a sarcastic laugh. "I'm not surprised."

We sat in awkward silence. It was a foreign feeling for us. I'd never felt like I couldn't just divulge every thought I had to Jen. She was the person I trusted the most.

"I don't have to go," I offered. "I was looking for an excuse not to. His grams invited me, and I just figured it would be rude to say no."

"Why would you say that?"

"I don't know." I did know. I just didn't know how to tell her. Even thinking about telling her that I might kind of like a man she once thought she'd marry someday made me want to hurl.

"Of course, you should go, Dee. I would never ask you not to. It'd be like turning down a dinner invitation from the first lady. The Monroes are good people and I'm glad they're taking you under their wings. Not everyone gets an invite to Sunday dinner."

"Okay," I sighed. "If you're sure."

"Devin?"

"Hmm?" My voice cracked even with a simple hum.

"Are you two...you *know*?"

"No! We're just friends!"

That sounded like a lie even to my ears. Not to mention, it was absurd to use that line with Jenna. She'd used it herself for many years. But as far as I knew, they never even kissed. He'd been an epic crush of hers for as long as I could remember.

"It's okay if you are, Dee. I wouldn't be upset with you." There was amusement in her tone.

I was surprised at how blasé she sounded. It's not that I thought she still had a thing for him or anything. She loved her husband. I just figured it'd be weird for her. Maybe I'd been worrying for nothing. But her feelings weren't the only thing holding me back.

"If you're looking for a rebound and for a good time, then Wes is your guy," she went on. "He's the perfect guy for that. A bit of advice, though... Whether you're just friends or not, make sure to protect your heart. He's an easy guy to fall for. He doesn't do it on purpose. I don't think he even realizes how many damaged hearts he's left in his wake. Even without all that humor and charm, he's one of the best guys I've known. I'm just not sure he's capable of fully giving himself to anyone. And I don't want to see you get hurt again, especially after everything you just went through with Noah."

"I know all this, Jen. It's exactly why friends is all I plan to be with him."

"Okay," she conceded with little faith in her voice.

A knock on my front door robbed me of the chance to reassure either one of us. I popped up off my bed, positive my ears were playing tricks on me. There was another knock. I glanced down at my lack of clothing. *Shit.*

"Jen, I have to go."

"Oh. Okay. I understand."

"No. I'm not upset with you. He's here and I'm still not dressed."

"Oh! Well, have fun. Be safe. And wear protection!"

"Oh my gosh, seriously, Jen. We aren't."

"Whatever you say. Later, tater."

"Bye, fry. Oh, and Jen..."

"Yeah?"

"I love you."

"Love you too, cuz."

I ended the call, tossing my phone on the bed. With another knock on the door, I tugged on the first thing I grabbed off my floor, hopping on one foot and stumbling into the wall as I made my way down the hall. After taking a quick glance downward to make sure all the important parts were covered, I flung the door open.

Wes stood there looking sinful. And gorgeous. His green eyes scanned me. His lips curved in amusement.

"Ready?"

"You're early," I accused.

"Does that mean you plan to change?"

Tucking my chin to my chest, I looked at the shirt I had on. It was a gag gift from Jenna years ago. It had two fried egg yolks strategically placed over each boob. "Nope," I deadpanned.

He shrugged, seemingly undisturbed. "Your call, sweetheart."

My mouth fell open. "I can't believe you'd seriously let me wear this to your family's Sunday dinner."

"Who doesn't like fried eggs? And those eggs look very appetizing, if you ask me," he added with a suggestive tone and his eyes glued to my boobs.

"Real cute, funny guy." I opened the door wider to allow him into my home. "Take a seat. I'll be ready in a few minutes."

He shrugged off his jacket, hanging it on the coat rack before picking up the remote to my TV and plopping onto the couch like he owned the place. Watching him make himself at home should've annoyed me. Instead, it warmed something inside of me that traveled straight to between my legs. Going to dinner with his family became less appealing than spending another night together on my couch.

We're only friends.

I repeated the words in my head as I marched back to my bedroom.

———

THE HOUSE WAS FILLED with warm laughter and mouthwatering smells as we walked into Grams' place. The boisterous chatter slowly faded as we entered the room. Lottie and Hannah were the first to greet me in a welcoming hug, quickly followed by Lily. Billy gave me a side hug before I was officially introduced to Grams, Tucker, and their father, Beau.

After all the introductions were out of the way and I'd personally thanked Grams for my chicken noodle soup, we migrated into the formal dining room.

"Everything looks great," I said to Grams, taking my seat next to Wes. "I can't believe this spread. You do this every week?"

"Don't let Grams fool you. We don't normally do things this fancy," Wes announced.

"Oh, hush up, you." She poked him in the rib with her finger. "And thank you, dear. It's nice to know my hard work is appreciated by someone."

Wes leaned to the side, his hand slipping onto my thigh, causing the hair on my nape to rise. His mouth hovered near my ear and I held my breath as he whispered in a low voice, "Kiss ass."

I shoved him back, puckering my lips as I blew him a mocking kiss while praying he didn't notice my reaction to his touch. He shook his head with a chuckle, removing his hand as he placed a cloth napkin in his lap.

The rest of the dinner, Wes continued to tease me with

his words and his touch. I was hyperaware of every move he made. I was constantly on edge, anxiously waiting for even the slightest touch, whether a brush of our legs, a playful nudge with his shoulder, or his breath feathering over my skin as he whispered in my ear to fill me in on the inside jokes being told at the table.

When I started to relax and return his flirting, Jenna's warning would ring loud in my ears, along with my own apprehensions. He made it so damn easy to look past one of the biggest warning bells. The deal breaker.

Part of me wished it didn't matter, wished I could just have casual sex and not get hurt. But I didn't work that way. And I was already growing attached to him, even without sex as a factor. My heart was too fragile and weak. It couldn't withstand a heartbreak the size of Texas—one that was guaranteed when it came to Wes Monroe.

12

WES

"Devin's pretty cool. What's the deal with you two?" Tucker asked as we stacked some more logs into the rusty, blue wheelbarrow.

Grams had sent the two of us and Billy outside to gather her some of the firewood she had stacked behind the shed. Another cold front was moving in and she wanted a fire for after dinner.

I glanced toward the house, where I could hear the muffled prattle of the women inside. "Nothing. We're friends."

Billy snickered from behind me. The man was gunning for a beating. Or unemployment. Maybe both.

I spun back around, biting my tongue before I fired him out of spite. Tucker stood stock-still, staring at me with a weird expression on his face.

"What?" I asked, immediately regretting it.

"You shittin' me right now?"

I shrugged. I didn't need Tucker in my business. "Why is that so hard for you dumbasses to believe?" I smirked. "Never mind. Answered my own question."

Tucker ignored my verbal jab, jerking his thumb toward the house. "I know how you look at the women you're friends with. And you're not looking at Devin like she's only a friend. Shit, I don't even think you look at the women you screw that way."

"*She* friend zoned *him*," Billy piped up.

My eyes darted to Billy. Sometimes, he was as bad as his sister Leighton when it came to keeping his mouth shut. "Hey, Miller, did Hannah ever tell you about that time I came to visit her in Seattle when you were out of town? I think it was about nine months ago, if I remember correctly."

His pupils flared. "Fuck you, man," he spat.

"I'll take that as a no." I winked.

"Not cool, dude," Tucker chuckled, shaking his head as he piled the last couple of logs on top.

"What's not cool is you two putting your noses where they don't belong."

They both gave me the same look. Their eyes narrowed as they crossed their arms over their chests, like synchronized dipshits.

Maybe I was a hypocrite. I'd done the same to them, sure, but *that* was completely different. They were both already in relationships with Lottie and Hannah—ones they would have fucked up for sure, had I not given them a little push. They should be thanking me, not looking at me like I was the asshole in this situation.

I gripped the handles of the wheelbarrow, lifting and rolling it back toward the house. I could feel their eyes boring into my back as I left them behind. I was done having this conversation. They were getting on my nerves. Mainly because I hated that they were both right. I wanted more. She didn't. End of story.

The women were all sitting in the den when I walked back in with my hands full of wood. And, if I was being honest, my pants full of wood too, thanks to little miss brown eyes bending over directly in front of me as I entered. Devin had her hands propped on her knees, her ass in the air as she positioned herself at eye level to talk to Lily.

She'd changed into a tight pair of jeans tucked into some brown riding boots and a thin, fitted sweater that left little to the imagination, even though every inch of her skin was covered. I blew out my cheeks, muttering a curse under my breath as I squeezed past where they stood in the middle of the only entry to the room. She popped up, her eyes wide as my semi-erect cock brushed against her ass. Served her right.

Devin's cheeks flushed a pretty pink as she looked over at me. Lily continued to babble, tugging at Devin's hand to regain her full attention. A heat flickered in her eyes before she returned them to Lily. The two of them moved out of the doorway as Billy and Tucker trudged inside with their own hands full of logs. Lily crawled into Grams' lap and Devin sat on the armrest of the couch near Hannah and Lottie. The three of them immediately struck up a conversation while Lottie held Colton in her arms, wrapped up in a blanket, sound asleep.

I passed the firewood off to my dad, who was already working on building a fire in the fireplace. Without a word between us, I stalked into the kitchen. I hadn't asked him if he needed a drink, because it didn't matter. I needed a reason to leave the room. And I'd never known the old man to turn one down when offered.

When I returned to the den, everyone had found their places. The only remaining spot was beside Devin on the love seat. As if that shit wasn't obvious. My family thought they'd play matchmaker. Fuck that.

I passed my dad the beer then stepped to the side, leaning a shoulder against the wall. I felt Devin's curious eyes on me, but I refused to meet them. I was done playing games. She wanted to be friends. Fine. We'd be friends. But I wasn't going to keep allowing that line to be blurred.

Being near her only made me want to reach for her. Touch her. Pull her into my arms. Somewhere between my conversation with Tucker and coming back in this room, I'd decided I needed to put an end to our flirting. I'd been doing a shit job of keeping my distance tonight. Now my whole family had the wrong impression.

"Wes, take a seat," Grams demanded.

I shook my head, jamming my hands in my pockets. "I'm good, Grams."

The whole room fell silent. Every pair of eyes in there

was suddenly on me, growing wide like I'd lost my damn mind. Maybe I had. Every pair, that was, except for Devin's. She sat there with no idea of the significance of my defiance.

I never disobeyed a request by Grams. None of us did. The woman was as sweet as honey, as loyal as they came, and as strong as an ox. When you stepped out of line, her bite was more lethal than a rattlesnake's.

I knew the storm that would be coming my way later. I could see it brewing in her gray-green eyes as her brows drew together. My face hardened with my resolve.

Devin cleared her throat, standing from the couch I refused to sit on. "Actually, I should be getting home. I have an early surgery scheduled for tomorrow morning."

The tension in the room had slowly shifted, but was still hanging on.

"Are you sure you can't stay for a bit longer?" Grams asked.

"No. I'm sorry to eat and dash. It was a lovely dinner and I appreciate you including me."

"Well, it was a pleasure finally meeting you, Devin," Dad chimed in, stepping forward to shake her hand. "It'll be nice having two vets in town."

Everyone followed Dad's lead telling Devin good-bye, ignoring me completely with the exception of Lily, who'd slipped off Grams' lap to run and hug my legs.

"Later, Lily-pad," I hugged her back, kissing the top of her head, before walking over to Lottie to give her a hug. I gently brushed the fuzzy hair on Colton's head, then faced Hannah.

She glared at me, crossing her arms over her round belly.

"I'd get up to give you a hug, but you aren't worth the effort," she stated sharply.

"Don't worry about it, City. I'm used to doing all the work in this relationship, anyway," I retorted, bending over to give her a hurried kiss on the cheek before she smacked me.

Grams was the caboose of the farewell train. I waited patiently as she pulled Devin in for a tight hug. "You're always welcome here. Whether for Sunday dinner or just dropping by for a glass of tea."

"Thank you, Mrs. Monroe."

"None of that. You call me Grams like the rest of them."

Devin's lips turned up in a soft smile with her chin still firmly tucked over Grams' shoulder. "Will do."

Grams pulled back from their hug, keeping her hands planted on each of Devin's shoulders as she looked her in the eye. "I mean it on both counts. You don't need an invitation and you can come with or without my good-for-nothing grandson."

Hands on my hips, I bowed my head with a light shake. She just had to get that final punch in. When I lifted my head, Devin had already moved to the front door and Grams had her eyes firmly on me, full of challenge. We hugged despite the current animosity between us.

"Get out of that stubborn head of yours, boy. It's time to smarten up and grow up. You're about to let a good thing pass you by," she warned in a low voice, for my ears only.

"Let it go. It's not happening," I grated. Apparently, I was on a roll tonight. Hell was already freezing over, no sense in holding back now. I kissed her warm cheek and then stalked out the door with Devin's short legs following hurriedly behind me.

————

"YOU WANT to tell me what that was all about?" Devin asked as we turned off the dirt drive and onto the main highway that led to town.

"You're gonna have to be more specific, Doc." I kept my eyes ahead, my jaw growing tight. I wasn't discussing this shit anymore tonight.

"I'm not an idiot, Wes. There was a lot of tension in that room, all because you refused to sit by me."

"What makes you think it had anything to do with you?"

"Okay. Fine," she huffed, tossing her hands up, landing them with a smack on her lap. "If you don't want to tell me why you're suddenly giving me the cold shoulder, that's fine. I'm not gonna make you. It's not like I didn't expect this."

"And what's that supposed to mean?"

"Don't play dumb, Wes," she scowled at my profile. "We both know this is what you do. You run. As soon as things get real for you, you run and never look back. Well you don't have to worry, cowboy. I'm not gonna tie you down. You can have all the space you want."

A torrent of anger rushed through me. I was tired of everyone thinking they knew me, knew what I wanted, knew what was best for me. "You don't know shit about me, Devin."

"I know more than you think," she muttered, crossing her arms and staring out the passenger window.

"That's right," I scoffed a humorless laugh, "because you and Jenna tell each other everything. Well, this may come as a surprise to you, but Jenna wasn't the expert on me. If she had been, she'd have known how I felt about her years before she met the dumbass she married."

"Pull over!"

"What?" I glanced over at her. She was a stretched rubber band, ready to snap, her nostrils flaring, her teeth grinding together. "No."

"I said, pull. *Over*."

"And I said, *no*."

"I want out. I'm not staying in this truck with you another damn minute while you treat me like crap and talk badly about my cousin and her husband."

"We're still miles from town. I'm not pulling over."

"I don't care! I'll walk!"

I ignored her. Her fist flew across the truck, nailing me in the arm. *Damn!* "What the hell was that?" I rubbed at the spot where she'd pegged me. That shit hurt.

"I'll kick your ass if you don't pull over right now."

I shifted my eyes between her and the road. From head to toe, I could see the war raging inside her—the same one raging in me. I yanked the wheel to the right, skidding to a stop on the graveled shoulder. I wasn't about to let her walk home, but both of us were too worked up for me to drive us safely. We both needed to cool the hell off.

As soon as I'd stopped, she was yanking on the handle

and jumping out of the truck. I dragged both hands over my face, taking a deep breath. Now would be a great time for God to answer at least one of my prayers and give me some damn patience. I was gonna need it with this woman.

With one final plea to God, I flung my door open. I marched toward where she'd stopped a few feet in front of the truck, my headlights shining on her back.

"Get back in the truck, Doc. You aren't walking home."

"I know," she declared, pulling her phone out of her purse.

I closed the distance between us as she searched for a signal. I snatched the phone from her hand, holding it over my head. She leapt for it, pointlessly. All she was managing to do was wear herself out. Which was fine by me.

"Ugh," she growled after her fifth failed attempt. "Give me my phone back."

"No. Get in the truck."

"I'll knee you in the balls again," she threatened. "And this time I won't even feel bad about it."

"I lived through it once. I can handle it. Now get in the damn truck."

She stared back at me, her eyes black with heat. "I hate you."

"Join the club."

"Fine. You win. Keep the damn phone," she said, turning in the opposite direction of the truck to walk toward town.

I stuffed her phone in my back pocket and snatched her wrist, spinning her into me. Her body slammed against mine and a surprised gasp escaped her lips. She stared up at me as

I pressed closer, until I could feel the erratic heart beat in her chest. My own heart started to play the same rhythm.

She was so damn gorgeous, especially when she was this worked up. She smelled like sunshine and felt like heaven in my arms. It infuriated the hell out of me.

I lowered my head, snaking one hand up the side of her neck until my fingers were weaving through her hair and palming the back of her head. Her breaths became more rapid and heavy the closer we got. "I'm done playing games, brown eyes," I rasped.

Her mouth opened to speak, but I didn't give her the chance. I smashed my lips to hers, swallowing her words, knowing all bets were off. It was almost instant, the way she succumbed to my intrusion. There was only a slight tug of war before she was giving in, moaning into the kiss, her nails digging into my chest as she clung to my shirt. She relented, sliding her hands up and around my neck, opening her mouth farther. I dove in, our tongues battling it out the same way we had been since the day we met.

This was one battle I was happy to fight. It wasn't enough, though. I needed more.

This woman was like an organ I couldn't live without. She was vital. That realization nearly had me breaking away, putting a stop to it all. But when she whimpered at the loss of pressure, I surged deeper.

I gripped her ass, lifting her into my arms as she wrapped her legs around my waist, our mouths barely parting. Taking the few steps to my truck, I pressed her into the hood. When she gasped at the contact, my name a breathy plea on her lips, my brain shut down and my dick took over. I moved from her lips to her neck, my hand slipping under the hem of her shirt and gliding over her hot skin. I was ready to rip off her clothes in the middle of the damn road and take her on the hood. Had it not been for the flashing lights coming up behind my truck, I might have done just that.

13

DEVIN

"Shit," Wes growled, pulling away.

I was tempted to beg, convince, force him not to stop, until I realized why he had. Red and blue lights flashed across his face as he stared behind me like a deer in headlights. I wiggled in his arms, needing him to release me. The last thing I wanted was someone to see me in a compromising position in the middle of the freaking highway with Wes Monroe locked between my legs.

That hadn't occurred to me moments ago, though. I was too wrapped up in his kiss, his touch. The way he claimed me like I belonged to him. My cheeks burned as he looked back down at me, his hold slowly loosening as I slid onto my own two feet.

"Let me handle this," he said, his voice full of grit.

I nodded. I wasn't in any state to speak to an officer anyway.

"Wes?" a voice hollered from the squad car, a door shutting in the process. I'd hoped to hear Deputy Roger's voice, but it wasn't.

I watched Wes for any sign. The slack of relief in the set of his shoulders told me he recognized the man.

"Yeah," he responded, then looked back at me. "Stay here," he ordered, stepping away.

I nodded once again, biting down on my lip. I wasn't worried about going to jail or getting a ticket. Wes would take care of getting rid of the sheriff. And that's exactly what worried me. We'd almost gone too far until we were interrupted.

A cold breeze picked up as Wes walked toward the car. Shivering and rubbing my hands down my arms, I strained to hear the muted conversation of their deep voices, with little success. There were few words exchanged. A small chuckle from the officer and a bro shake and clap on the back before the flashing lights were off and the car was pulling away.

Wes strolled back over, his hardened exterior in place once again. His eyes did a quick inspection of me from head to toe before they were fixed back on mine. "Get in the truck, Doc." His voice was firm, leaving no room for argument. Turning his back to me, he climbed into his truck, slamming the door.

I let out a resigned sigh, doing the same.

———

IF I THOUGHT the tension before our kiss couldn't have been more suffocating, I was proven wrong on the remainder of the drive to my house. The bite in the air was no match for the frigid shoulder Wes was giving me.

He hadn't spoken a word to me since we got back in the truck, hadn't spared me a single glance. He drove as if I wasn't sitting a few feet away, silently falling apart. I'd been so wrapped up in my internal destruction, I hadn't even noticed we'd stopped in front of my house.

It wasn't until I heard his heavy sigh and his head falling back on the headrest that I was snapped out of my own head. The awkward silence continued. I told myself I needed to just get the hell out and inside before any more damage was done. But I couldn't. I couldn't walk away without clearing the air.

"Wes," I pleaded.

"Stop overthinking it, Doc."

"I can't."

He lifted his head. "I'm not a puzzle you need to figure out. I say what I mean, and I mean what I say. I'm done playing games. I don't do relationships. And being just friends is off the table. It's your choice. You know where I stand."

"I'm not sure I can do that." My gut twisted, spurring tears to well in my eyes.

"I understand. And I'd never ask you to do something you're not comfortable with. If you change your mind, you have my number."

Ripping his eyes from mine, he stared out the windshield, his hands firmly on the wheel. He was done. Done with this conversation. Done with me, unless I wanted to give him more than friendship. But he wasn't willing to give me more than just friends with benefits. It was bullshit. Whatever guilt or sadness I'd felt moments ago was gone with that understanding.

"Don't hold your breath," I hissed, flinging the door open and slamming it in his face. I ran up the porch steps and barreled through the front door, slamming it for good measure. After twisting the lock, I pressed my back against it, tears of anger now falling. I waited for the sound of his truck to leave.

For the briefest moment, I wondered if he'd come after me. I hated that I wanted him to, and hated that I knew for sure he wasn't, finally confirmed by the sound of his tires squealing as he peeled off.

14

"Damn it!" I smacked an open palm against the steering wheel when Devin's front door slammed shut.

I'd messed up.

Royally.

I never should've fucking kissed her. But I was tired of fighting it, tired of pretending there was nothing there between us. I took one final glance at her dark house, then tore off before I did something else stupid. Like pound on the door and beg her to forgive me.

———

I SNIFFED at the carton of old food, my face twisting up at the smell. I shoved it back in and slammed the fridge door shut.

A smack came to the back of my head.

What the...?

I jerked around to look behind me, rubbing my hand where the sting radiated from. Hannah stood there looking more pissed than I'd ever seen before.

"I'm not in the mood, City," I warned her. I was starving and tired. Tired of every woman in my life right now feeling the need to hit and lecture me. I was a grown-ass man. I'd make my own damn decisions.

"Good. Because neither am I."

"What are you doing here?"

"I came to smack some sense into you. Did it work?"

"Nope." I planted my hands on my hips. "Feel free to go now."

She tossed a greasy, brown paper bag onto the counter beside me. My mouth watered. "What's in the bag?"

"A burger from Kathy's. Billy said Grams cut you off."

For once I was glad Billy couldn't keep his big mouth shut. It'd been two weeks since I'd had a home-cooked meal. Grams had turned me away from her door when I showed up for lunch with Billy the Monday after the shit show of a Sunday dinner. And worse than cutting me off from her cooking, she was giving me the silent treatment. I'd much rather her yell and smack me around like the rest of them. At least then I wouldn't be hungry.

She'd never gone this long without forgiving me. I didn't understand her hang up on Devin, or why she was pushing so hard for me to pursue things with her. She'd never much cared what I did in my personal life before. Sure, she'd given me a hard time about my philandering. But that's all it ever was.

I reached for the bag.

"Nope." Hannah snatched it away just before I got to it, holding it behind her back.

Normally, I'd go after it, knowing I could easily overpower her. But she was pregnant, and I wasn't going to risk even accidentally hurting her or the baby.

Folding my arms across my chest, I sighed, a headache pushing its way to the front. "Fine. Let's get this over with. Say what you came to say and then leave."

"You're an idiot."

"Noted."

"And the most stubborn, annoying man I've ever met. And that's saying a lot, considering how many I've met."

I nodded. She wasn't saying anything she hadn't told me before. Though, most of the time she hadn't delivered the words with so much genuine anger and disappointment behind them. "You done?"

When I gave her little emotion, her body deflated like a balloon. "Yes. But we aren't. Now sit down and start talking." She pointed to a stool at my breakfast bar.

"I'm gonna take a pass."

"No, you aren't. Not if you want this burger. I can hear your stomach growling from here. So, what's it gonna be?"

I dropped my arms, taking a seat on one of the barstools. Hannah moved to join me. She tossed the bag on the counter in front of me and then proceeded to hoist herself up onto a stool. As she struggled, I found myself cracking a smile for the first time in weeks. The memory of our initial meeting came rushing to the forefront of my mind.

"Need some help?" I asked, with a full-blown grin now.

"Shut up," she scowled, nearly out of breath, finally settling her butt into the seat next to me.

I opened the bag and pulled out the burger. I took a big-ass bite, taking little time to chew before swallowing. I'd been too busy to get groceries or even head into town for a lunch break. I'd been eating whatever scraps of food I could find for the last few weeks, which wasn't much.

"You look like shit, by the way," she announced.

I shrugged. She could insult me all she wanted if she promised to keep bringing me food.

She stopped my wrists as I lifted to take another bite. "We had a deal."

"What do you want to know?"

"Why you're acting like an epic jackass. I mean, more so than usual. You like Devin."

"Never said I didn't."

"Then why does she look like someone kicked one of her sick puppies these last few weeks. She'll barely hang out with Lottie and me. She turned us down on our last girls' night."

"How should I know? Maybe she doesn't like hanging out with you."

She smacked me again.

"Woman. Will you stop that?"

"Stop making me feel the need to."

I dropped the burger, suddenly losing my appetite.

"Look. I don't know why Devin's upset or avoiding you guys," I lied. "And frankly, I don't care."

I did care. And that was the damn problem. Two weeks of staying away from her had only made my life more miserable. I'd even forced myself to go out and pick up another woman in a bar. But by the time I got there, the last thing I wanted to do was talk to or touch another woman who wasn't Devin. She'd ruined me with one damn kiss.

"You're lying."

"How would you know?"

"Because we're besties, remember?"

"Well, at least you finally admit it," I grumbled, sitting back.

She sighed, twisting in her seat to face me, her belly nearly knocking me out of my chair.

"Watch it with that thing, will ya?"

She narrowed her eyes. "Tell me why you're set on not giving this thing a chance."

"Who says it's me? I offered her more. She's the one who said no."

"Did you offer her more, or just your dick?"

"We both know that's all I'm good for."

"I don't know the size of your dick and don't care to." She raised a hand to silence me when I opened my mouth. "But I do know you have a big heart, Wes. You just refuse to share it with most."

I picked at my burger, refusing to respond. She exhaled, nudging me in the shoulder. "Do you remember what you told me that night at Tucker and Lottie's? The night I was leaving for Seattle and was set on ignoring Billy."

I kept quiet.

"You're repeating history."

"We aren't you and Billy."

"I didn't mean our history. I meant yours. Your advice came from your past. You never told me what it was, but I can put the pieces together and guess."

"And what do you think happened?"

"You let someone you cared about get away."

I nodded.

"Don't do it again."

"It's not that easy, City."

"It is."

"That someone was Devin's cousin."

Her mouth opened in a giant "O" as she sat back in her chair, resting her hands on her belly, letting this new revelation soak in. "Do you—"

"No," I answered immediately.

I knew what she was thinking: that I still had feelings for Jenna. I didn't. I hadn't for years. I'd figured out a long time ago we weren't meant to be. It took me awhile to understand that, and maybe part of me always wondered whether I'd just convinced myself of it. But as soon as I met and spent some time with Devin, I knew I'd never felt this way before.

With Jenna, I never had a problem being with other girls while I waited for our chance. With Devin, I could barely look at another woman, much less touch one.

"Then what's holding you back?" she asked, her voice softening.

"You know I don't do relationships."

The rest of my reason I kept to myself. Devin deserved more than just a few nights in my bed. I'm not capable of giving her that. She made the right choice walking away from me the other night. I knew that. She knew that. That was why it fucking hurt so much.

"That's bullshit, and I refuse to believe it."

"Doesn't matter what you believe."

"Say I feed into this crap...then why? Give me one reason why you refuse to do relationships."

The reason was easy. With the exception of Grams, every damn woman I'd ever cared for, I'd lost. My mother and sister both died. Jenna, though mostly by my doing, was no longer in my life, either. But I wasn't about to say any of that out loud.

I stood from my seat, wrapping up the burger and tossing it back in the bag.

"Where are you going?"

"Back to work."

"We aren't done."

"We are. I don't need you to fix me, Han. I'm fine the way I am."

"That's not what I'm trying to do. I'm just trying to understand your side of things."

I walked to the trash, dropping the bag inside. "I gotta go. We're behind schedule as it is." Another lie. But it was the only way to get her off my back.

"Fine." She stood from her seat. As she reached for her purse, she doubled over, clutching her stomach with a hiss.

"Han?" I ran to her side. "What's wrong? Is it the baby?"

"I'm fine." She took a few deep breaths, trying to right herself. "It's just Braxton Hicks or something like that."

"I'll drive you to the hospital."

"No. I said I'm good."

"I'm driving you home then. I'll call Billy to meet us at the house."

"I said I was fine, Wes," she gritted through her teeth as she bit through more pain.

"Yeah, well I'm not taking any chances. If something happened to you, I'd never forgive myself and Billy would kick my ass." Not that he'd need to. "Let's go, City." I put my hand on her back, taking her purse as I helped her to my truck. For once, she allowed me the privilege.

———

AFTER CALLING Billy and dropping Hannah at their house, I headed to Dudley's. The rest of the work day was shot, and I needed a drink after my conversation with Hannah.

Timmy was already cracking a beer open for me by the time I took a seat in the nearly empty joint.

"Thanks, man," I said as he slid the bottle into my hand.

"Surprised to see you here this early." He picked up a rag and started wiping down an already impeccably clean bar top.

"Quit early today."

"That explains what you're doing here early. Doesn't explain why you look like shit."

"Work's been rough."

"Sure. I believe that."

"Don't you start, too. I came here to get away from all the sage advice."

He tossed his rag to the side. "I get it. Not here for advice. How about a drinking buddy?" He pulled out another bottle of beer, popping the top. He leaned against the bar in front of me, taking a long, drawn-out sip.

I cocked an eyebrow. "Drinking on the job now?"

"I'm making a one-time exception. Besides, shit doesn't start gettin' busy 'round here for another four hours."

We clanked the necks of our bottles and spent the next few hours talking about all kinds of random shit, as usual. When newcomers started filing in, he sighed, tossing his second empty bottle in the trash.

"Looks like it's go time, man."

I nodded, taking another pull of my beer. "You know, you should really get some help 'round here."

He scoffed, picking up a bar rag and draping it on his shoulder. "Tell you what. You don't tell me how to run my business, and I won't tell you what a colossal idiot you are for not making things right with the Doc."

"And what do you know about that?"

"More than I care to. She was in here a few nights ago."

I thought I was doing a damn fine job not showing any reaction to that news, but from the tilt of Timmy's lips, I wasn't.

"Don't worry, man. I kept an eye on her. She only had a few shots and seemed more concerned about talking music and asking me questions about you than taking any interest in the guys who were trying to buy her drinks."

I nodded my appreciation. "Thanks, man."

"Don't mention it." A couple of ladies walked up to the bar, drawing his attention. "Duty calls. You good?"

"Yeah. Just get me the tab when you get a chance."

"Don't worry about it. It's on the house." He walked off, not giving me the opportunity to argue. As he mixed their cocktails, I felt their eyes on me. I ignored them, standing from the stool and pulling out my wallet. I tossed a couple of twenties on the bar and took off.

———

"Hello," I answered my phone as I turned left at the court-house to head home.

"Hey..."

My foot let off the gas when I heard Devin's timid voice through my speakers. I glanced over at my phone for confir-mation it was really her. I hadn't paid attention to who was calling when I picked up.

"I didn't expect you to answer. I thought you might be out tonight," she continued.

"Then why did you call?" I pulled my truck to the side of the road, my heart pounding like the pussy it was in my chest. I didn't know how to take this unexpected call. Was she giving in? Was she good with being fuck buddies? Why was I not feeling okay with that? I should be freaking ecstatic right now.

"I don't know..." She went quiet, and I imagined she was nibbling on those pouty lips the way she did when she was nervous.

"You're going to have to do better than that, Doc."

She sighed with annoyance. "I have a plumbing issue."

"You do know my brother is the contractor, not me."

"Yeah. It's not that kind of plumbing issue..."

I flipped the truck around, heading back into town with a grin on my face. "I'll be there in five."

————

DEVIN OPENED the door looking worse for wear, but still beautiful as hell. I guess they hadn't been lying about her state. I was immediately pissed at myself, knowing I had a part in it.

Without even a hello, she turned her back to me and walked away, leaving the door wide open. When I didn't make a move, she glanced over her shoulder. "Are you coming?"

Shit. Was this how it was gonna go down? Not that I'd ever felt the need to have drawn-out conversations with the women I slept with before, but this was a bit forward even for me. I figured we'd clear the air first, make sure we were on the same page. But she seemed set on heading straight to the bedroom and getting down to business.

15

DEVIN

Wes stood in my doorway, his brows pinching, a frown on his face. Maybe this was a bad idea. It took me hours to work up the nerve to call him. I'd pulled up his number at least ten times before I finally connected the call.

But what else was I supposed to do? I couldn't sleep. I needed him.

"Wes?"

His eyes snapped to mine. "Yeah?"

"It's this way." I jabbed my thumb down the hall.

He nodded, but still didn't move.

"You okay?" I asked.

He lowered his head, rubbing at the back of his neck. "Yeah, it's just—"

"If you changed your mind, it's fine. I can call someone else."

"It'd be that easy for you, huh?" His faced hardened with his question, his fist opening and closing.

"Well, no... Not exactly. You were kind of my last option."

"Wow. You really know how to kill a man's ego. I'm surprised you called me at all."

"Well, I'm not gonna be able to sleep until it's taken care of." I sighed, crossing my arms, kicking out a hip. "You know what, just forget it. This was a mistake."

"I'm not saying I won't help you with your *situation*. I just... Shit, can you give me a minute?" He rubbed his hand down over his mouth as he looked at me from head to toe.

If I knew he was going to be this annoyed about it, I never would have called him. "Fine. Whatever." I tossed my hands up, stomping down the hall.

He muttered another curse before trudging slowly behind me. I stopped at the doorway to the bathroom, keeping as much distance as I could while I looked for the little sucker. He was nowhere to be found, but I knew he was still in there. Or at least I hoped.

"What are we doing?" Wes whispered over my shoulder, sending a shudder down my back. His cologne overpowered the air around me.

I nudged him back with my elbow.

"In there." I pointed into the bathroom.

"That's where you want to do this?" He tipped his head to the side, rubbing at his jaw as he contemplated for a moment. He shrugged, coming to some sort of decision. "Okay, then. Lead the way."

"Uh-uh." I shook my head. "You're on your own. No way in hell am I going in there with you."

"What do you mean?"

"I'm not touching that thing."

He puffed out his cheeks, releasing a breath, running his fingers through his hair. "You're making it really hard for me to perform when you keep throwing those kinds of comments my way."

"Sorry." I shrugged. "But I'm staying right here while you take care of business in there. I'm fine watching."

His eyes widened as they looked from me to the bathroom. "You're full of surprises, brown eyes. I never expected this."

I shrugged, shoving him forward into the bathroom. "Go on. I'd like to sleep at some point tonight."

He exhaled again, walking into the bathroom, and then turned to face me. "I gotta admit this is a little unusual, even for me. Not that I don't kind of like it, but I'm feeling a little stage fright right now. How do you want me to do this?"

"I guess we should find it first."

He chuckled, reaching for the snap on his pants. "That shouldn't be a problem." Before I could register what was going on, he was unzipping his pants.

"What the hell are you doing?" I screamed.

He stopped, flinging his arms out to the side. "I don't know! This was your fucking idea!" He stared back at me, planting his hands on his broad hips, confusion etched all over his face.

I blinked, the shock slowly fading as I stared at his

disgruntled expression. "Oh— Oh my God." My hands flew to my mouth as I tried to hold back a laugh, everything finally dawning on me. "You thought—oh my God." I bent over in a fit of laughter.

I tried to stop. I really did. But I couldn't. Especially when he was still standing there with his fly open, looking out of sorts.

"You're a weird chick, Doc." He zipped up his pants. "I'm not so sure what's so funny right now, but I can guarantee you my dick is nothing to laugh about."

"Wes, I'm sorry," I tried to apologize through my laughter. "I think you got the wrong idea. I didn't call you here to"—I waved a hand toward his crotch—"you know..." I stared at it, noticing how hard it was. And big. A flash of heat trickled south.

Wes cleared his throat and my eyes traveled upward, where a slow smile was building on his face as I did.

"Are you sure about that?"

I had no idea how he'd managed to shift the embarrassment from himself to me so quickly. "No—I mean, yes." Tilting my head back, I blew out a breath. "I mean yes, I'm sure. No, I didn't call you here to—can we just move on?"

"Whatever you say, Doc. Then what 'plumbing issue' did you have?" he asked skeptically.

"A scorpion. There was one between the tub and the toilet when I came in here earlier."

"A scorpion?" He glanced over to where I'd claimed to have seen it. "Are you sure?"

"Yes, I'm sure! And I won't be able to sleep until I know it's gone."

"Well, it's not there now."

"It's in here somewhere. I've been keeping an eye on the doorway since I ran out of it." I took one step in to peer around him at the spot where I'd originally spotted the nasty thing.

He was right. It wasn't there.

"Where did it go?" I huffed, putting my hands on my hips as I looked back at him.

He didn't answer. He just stared unblinking, his face paling and his eyes slowly widening as he looked slightly over my head.

"Wes?" My voice cracked with my racing heart.

"Don't. Move," he slowly and sternly warned me.

I snapped my eyes closed, every muscle in me going rigid. "Wes?"

"Shhh...just hold still."

"Tell me it's not on me!"

"It's not on you. It's on the wall right above you."

Without another thought, I screamed and sprinted out of the room and down the hall. There was no way in hell I was waiting for that thing to drop onto my head. Wes' booming laughter roared and echoed from behind me.

He was still laughing as he walked down the hall to where I'd stopped to freak out. I squirmed and spun, rubbing my hands all over as I tried to rid my body of the imaginary creepy crawlers on it.

"Got ya." He winked, crossing his arms.

I stopped. His words registered, and I narrowed my eyes. "That's not funny!" I screeched.

"It was for me," he said laughing, a wicked gleam in his green eyes.

"You're an ass." I shoved at his chest as he closed in on me, trapping me in a hug, the heat of his body enveloping me. His laughter vibrated through his chest and against my cheek, causing another shot of warmth to course through me. I loved being around this Wes. The light and fun one.

"Oh, come on, Doc. You kind of deserved it after letting me think you wanted me to jack off in front of you."

My smile cracked and I chuckled against him, burying my face against his hard pecs. "I can't believe you were actually going to do it."

"There's not much I wouldn't do for you," he confessed in a low voice.

We both stilled, our laughter silenced by his admission. It was no longer the prominent vibration I felt as I remained pressed against him. Instead, it was the frantic rhythm of his heartbeat mimicking mine.

After a few more beats of silence, I lifted my head to meet his gaze. His eyes were soft, the honesty in his words visible in them.

"I'm not like the other girls. I can't be. I *won't* be."

"I know."

"And I'm not *her*."

My biggest fear was out of my lips and in the air, floating between us. As soon as I said it, I realized it was the only thing holding me back. I wanted him. I knew he wanted me. But I wanted him to want me for me.

"I know. She's not who I want. There's no one else I want. Just you."

"And what happens when we cross this line? What do you expect at the end of this?"

He brushed a hand across my cheek, his lids heavy as he focused on my lips. "To make you forget *he* ever existed."

The sound of his deep, sexy voice pulled me under, the promise of his words something I was desperate for. Without another thought my lips were on his, my hands greedily wrapping around his neck, pulling him tighter to me. The tips of his fingers dug into my waist as he pressed against me, stepping me backward and flush against the wall. He groaned against my lips. I opened them more and his tongue swooped in, caressing mine in a heated kiss.

I gasped when his hands dropped, digging into my ass, squeezing, and lifting. "Wes," I whimpered, hiking one leg up, climbing him like a tree.

Taking my thigh in his hand, he hoisted me up until I had both legs wrapped around his waist. The hard ridge in his jeans pressed deeper into me, forcing another desperate moan to emit from deep in my throat.

He jerked back, burying his face in my neck. "Doc," he rasped, his heavy breaths against my skin. "We should stop."

"No," I blurted my breathy insistence.

"Are you sure?"

I nodded.

"I need to hear you say it."

"Yes. I am," I assured him, still nodding.

He lifted his head, his eyes searching mine for what felt like forever. I'd felt the shift in his frame, saw the hesitation in his eyes as he began to doubt my words. "Fuck," he sighed, dropping his lips back to mine with a quick kiss.

"Wes." I cupped his face in my palms, tightening my legs at his waist, and forced him to look at me again. "Please. I want this."

Using one arm and the wall to hold me up, he lifted his other hand, combing it through my hair. "I know, brown eyes. But not like this."

"Yes. Just like this. It's exactly what I need." I pleaded with my eyes, hoping he saw the sincerity there, rather than the desperation.

I meant every word. I had no expectations of a future with him. We wanted the same thing: an incredible night that would make me forget every mistake I'd made the last four years.

His head fell, his forehead pressing to mine as I locked my hands at the back of his neck. He rolled it back and forth, fighting an internal battle as he struggled with his decision. When he pressed a sweet kiss to the top of my head, I felt the rejection.

But then he hiked me higher on his body, getting a good grip as he stepped us away from the wall. "As much as I'd like to fuck you up against this wall, I won't. I'm gonna do at least one thing right tonight. Where's the bed?"

I tucked my lips between my teeth, failing to contain my smile. "First door on your left."

He kissed me again, carrying me as he walked to the bedroom. He lowered me to the bed and I released my hold on him, scooting back toward the headboard. I propped myself up on my elbows, watching as he reached a hand behind his back, tugging his shirt over his head and tossing it to the floor.

I tried not to gawk at the defined ripples in his abs. He flicked the button on his jeans, unzipping them with a smirk. "You planning on just watching again?"

"Maybe." My lips pursed with a smile as I teased him.

He dropped his pants, and my attempts not to salivate were long forgotten. The man was naked. And hard. Everywhere.

The mattress dipped. He gripped my ankles with a fast tug, causing my elbows to fall and my head to plop back on the pillow. He crawled over me using a knee to spread my legs wide, his lips nearing my ear. "Maybe next time."

My breath caught. Shivers rolled through me. I tried not to think about him wanting a next time with me. I knew it wasn't a promise. There were levels to his seduction. His verbal teasing was the first. His hot mouth pressing kisses against my sensitive skin was the next. The rough gentleness of his hands as he stripped me naked took me higher and higher. And when his tongue licked and sucked between my legs, I was soaring toward the penthouse.

My eyes closed, rolling back in my head, my hands fisting the sheets as I felt myself free-falling and gasping his name. He planted one last kiss inside my thigh before lifting his head. My chest heaved as I sucked in as many breaths as I could, my body still soaring with the remnants of my orgasm and a new anticipation.

He pushed up, sitting back on his knees, that heart-melting grin on his face and a sexy glint in his eyes. "I could do that all day long."

I laughed, doubting his words. He smiled wider, then reached for his jeans. Finding his wallet, he tossed them back to the floor. Still kneeling between my legs, he pulled out a condom and rolled it on within seconds. It was sexy as hell watching him and the way every one of his muscles seemed to flex and bulge as he moved.

The whole time he did, his eyes were on me, his face consumed with an emotion I didn't expect. I told myself I was misreading it, that I was looking for more when I knew it wasn't there. My heart and eyes were only playing tricks on me.

He gripped the backside of my knees, spreading me wider. He sent shivers through me and goosebumps across my skin as he peppered it with kisses. I lifted my hips, begging for him. He ignored my desperation and continued to tease me with his mouth and hands, sliding them up my stomach and to my breasts, giving every piece of me equal attention. Then his lips brushed mine with an unexpected tenderness.

"Last chance, Doc," he rasped into my neck.

There was no way I was changing my mind. I reached between us, gripping his hard length, and lining it with my entrance.

He didn't force a verbal response from me this time. He

slid into me with ease, digging his fingers into my left thigh as he lifted to his other arm. His eyes closed. His nostrils flared as he took a deep inhale. I tilted my hips, grinding them against him.

"You're gonna be the death of me," he growled, his control slipping. Pulling back, he pumped back in harder. Again, and again. His pace increasing.

I moaned between thrusts, which only seemed to encourage his fervor, each one becoming more punishing, pulling us both over. His body tensed as mine convulsed beneath him.

"Fuck," he roared, burying his face in my neck once again.

I felt him pulse inside me as I clenched around him a few more times. Lifting to his elbows, he dotted my skin with soft kisses. This time, I was greeted with a lazy grin on his face as he gazed at me. I immediately decided it was my favorite.

"If you keep looking at me like that, we'll be going for round two," he warned.

"And going again is a problem for you?"

"Nope. Just not sure you're ready for what I have planned next time."

"It must've been good, if you're already planning our future," I teased and then clamped my lips shut, hoping my words hadn't scared him off.

Giving me a soft smile, he kissed my lips before rolling off me and out of the bed, leaving me alone in the room while he discarded the condom. I covered my face with my arm, wishing I'd learn to keep my big mouth shut.

The bed dipped beside me and I felt his hand at my wrist, tugging it away from my face.

"Get out of your head, Doc."

I sighed and nodded.

"You hungry?"

"A little," I admitted. I hadn't had dinner, since I'd spent most of the evening camping out on watch for the scorpion.

Taking my hands, he pulled me from the bed before slipping on his jeans. I almost hated to see him dressed again. But when he started to stride out of my room, barefoot and shirtless, with his jeans hanging low on his hips, leaving me tingling all over, I decided I could live with it.

I slipped into a clean pair of panties and an oversized tee before following him into the kitchen. He was already searching through my fridge, pulling out a carton of eggs, bread, and butter.

"Breakfast for dinner?" I asked.

"Yep." He spun to look at me, stopping in his tracks. His eyes did an achingly slow scan before he cleared his throat. "How do you feel about an egg sandwich?"

"Sounds good to me." I grinned, glad I wasn't the only one having difficulty controlling myself.

"Good, because it's one of the few things I know how to cook." He put the items on the counter next to the stove.

I laughed, opening a cabinet door, pulling out a couple of frying pans. I placed them on the stove before retrieving the non-stick spray, sliced cheddar cheese, and a package of bacon to cook.

We worked simultaneously beside each other, him manning the eggs and toast, while I fried up some bacon.

"What do you do for food if you don't cook?"

"Grams."

"Ah. Of course." I smiled.

"Except, she's still not too happy with me after our Sunday dinner. So, I've been living off PB&Js lately."

"You could always apologize." I playfully bumped my hip against his.

He flipped the eggs, glancing over at me. "Tried that after the first meal she banned me from."

"Well, what do you normally do?"

"What do you mean?"

"You know..." I shrugged. "Like when you normally mess up."

He stopped, his face frowning as he set the spatula to the side. He crossed his arms, turning to face me. "What makes you think I've messed up before?"

"Oh, come on. Seriously?" I chuckled, glancing over at him, surprised by the offense on his face. "Oh. You are serious."

He quirked an eyebrow.

"I didn't mean to offend you, but we're talking about you here."

"I'm aware. This may come as a surprise to you, but I'm not as bad of a guy as you think."

"I'm sorry. That came out wrong. I don't think you're a bad guy."

He gave me a silent look before turning back to the eggs.

Despite the skepticism on his face, I truly meant it. I knew he wasn't a bad guy. He was just emotionally unavailable for some unknown reason.

I removed the last of the cooked bacon from the pan and turned off the heat. Wes snatched the toast from the toaster and began to assemble the first sandwich, passing it off to me so I could layer the cheese and bacon. We worked together, as if we'd done it a million times before.

With our plates in hand, we sat on opposite ends of the couch to eat in comfortable silence. I studied him, my naturally inquisitive mind demanding to know more.

He was an enigma.

A contradiction.

A confident man, but not as big of a jerk as one would expect, given his reputation.

He was caring and considerate and loyal to his friends and family, almost to a fault. He did relationships well, as long as they were platonic.

It made no sense to me.

"Can I ask you something?" I took the final bite of my sandwich and set my plate aside.

"Shoot."

"Don't take this the wrong way, I'm just curious. Why the no-relationship stance?"

His neck stiffened, the cords standing out as he leaned forward, setting his own plate down on the coffee table. He hung his head, with his elbows resting on his knees, his palms rubbing over his face.

I reached for him, ready to tell him to forget it. It was

obvious there wasn't an easy explanation. I didn't want to push him, afraid he'd withdraw from me and ice me out once again. As my hand touched his shoulder and his eyes flicked to mine, I closed my mouth, shocked by the worry I saw in them.

16

I wished I had an easy answer for her. Wished I could admit to her that the defining moment had been when I walked away from Jenna. I already knew how she'd interpret that if I did.

She'd regret sleeping with me. It was the last thing I wanted her to feel. She'd think I was still hung up on Jenna.

That wasn't the case, though. My heart was already beyond repair, my resolve had been hardening well before Jenna. She was just one tiny fissure in it. The first cracks started after my mom's death. I'd thought Jenna might've been able to repair it at one point, thought I needed her to be the one to do it. But when my younger sister Jamie died, it finally shattered completely.

The fact that I'd never felt anything for any of the women I'd been with only reinforced my determination. But damn if

I wasn't suddenly questioning everything I thought I knew and wanted.

I opened my mouth, unsure exactly what it was I was going to say. My phone rang in my pocket, interrupting us. I pulled it out, seeing Tucker's name, and hit decline, tossing it in front of me.

"You can answer that." She glanced at where it clattered onto the table.

"I'll call him back."

It immediately started to ring again. I cursed under my breath, ready to hit ignore again until I saw the name flashing on the screen.

Dad.

I picked it up with a sinking feeling in my stomach. My dad hardly ever called. The last time I had back-to-back phone calls from Tucker and him was one of the worst days of my life.

I answered the call, putting the phone to my ear without a word.

"Wes?"

"Yeah."

"Where are you?"

"In town. What is it?"

"It's Grams. You need to get to the hospital."

———

I SHOVED through the hospital doors, nearly running a guy over. Devin was hot on my heels, chasing after me. She'd insisted on coming and I didn't have time to waste on arguing with her.

I didn't slow until I'd reached the ER reception desk. "Where is she?" I bellowed, startling the nurse behind the counter.

"Mr. Monroe, if you'll just take a seat with—"

"No. Not until I know where she is."

"Wes."

I turned at the sound of my dad's gruff voice. He stood in the waiting area with the rest of my family, Hannah, and Billy. They were all huddled with worry-stricken faces. I stared back at the nurse, wondering what she knew and wasn't saying. She ducked her head and answered the ringing phone beside her.

Devin's hand gently touched my bicep in support as she urged me forward to where my family was.

My father was the first to hug me, which only increased my fear. The man rarely showed emotion. He gave my back a couple rough pats before pulling away.

"What happened?" I asked, needing some answers.

"She was having chest pains when I stopped by to pick up the kids," Lottie spoke up. "She tried to brush it off, but I could tell she was moving slower than normal. I sent Tucker back over to check on her as soon as I got home."

"Shit." I pushed a hand through my hair, tugging at the strands as I looked over at Tucker. "Is she?"

"She's alive," he said, squeezing my shoulder. "We think it was the start of a heart attack. I got her here as fast as I could, and they took her back immediately. We're waiting for the doctor now."

I nodded. "Where are the kids?" I looked at Lottie again. "Does Lily know?"

"With Leighton and Aaron. I dropped them off at their house on my way here. She knows Grams isn't feeling well. That's all. I didn't want to scare her any more than necessary."

I absently nodded again.

"She's gonna be fine, Wes," Lottie tried to assure me as everyone else moved to reclaim their seats.

As much as I appreciated it, I knew better than to believe her. She had as much control as I did in ensuring that: zero.

"I'm gonna get some coffee. Does anybody need anything?" Devin spoke up for the first time.

All eyes went to her and then to me, most of them with questioning stares, as if they were just realizing she'd come with me. I shook my head at her, ignoring everyone else.

"I'll go with you," Billy volunteered. He gave Hannah a kiss on the head as he stood, then walked away with Devin in search of coffee.

I took his seat next to Hannah, resting my elbows on my knees. I felt her hand brush my back. "Hang in there, big guy. Grams is as tough as they come. She won't go down without a fight. If I had to bet, she'll pull through this and come out swinging on the other side."

I blew out a ragged breath, sitting back in the seat.

I hoped she was right. Losing Grams at any point in my life would be tough. But losing her when we hadn't been speaking for weeks, would make it nearly impossible for me to go on.

————

IT'D BEEN hours since we'd arrived. We were all exhausted, yet restless. When Dr. Matthews finally walked through the staff doors, Dad, Tucker, and I were all on our feet immediately.

"Dr. Matthews." Dad shook his hand as we approached from behind him.

"Beau," he responded. "I'm gonna get straight to it, since I know you've all got to be tired."

We nodded in unison, thankful he wasn't planning to beat around the bush.

"She had a minor heart attack, but she's okay and resting in a private room now."

"Can we see her?" I interrupted.

"Yes, but keep the visits short and minimal. Despite what she might think, she needs to rest."

Tucker and Dad both looked at me, giving me a silent nod to go first. I didn't stick around for the rest of the rundown from Dr. Matthews. After getting her room number, I darted through the hospital corridor, only slowing my pace when her room came into view.

I took a deep breath, shaking off the nerves as I turned the corner around the jamb. She was sitting up in her bed, perfectly content, watching the late-night news.

"You should be resting," I reprimanded, even though

seeing her looking mostly normal finally eased some of the worry.

Her eyes did a slow roll as she looked over at me. "If I needed you to give me free medical advice, I wouldn't be wasting all my money on that good for nothing Dr. Matthews."

"He saved your life."

She huffed, crossing her arms. "He's trying to kill me."

"I doubt that."

"I almost keeled over when he said I needed to cut back on my biscuits and sausage gravy. What kind of man did his momma raise? I'll be having a talk with her come Sunday."

"You're lucky you'll be seeing her on Sunday," I reminded her, pulling a chair next to her bed.

I took a seat, shaking my head with a small chuckle. Hannah was right. Despite the exhaustion in her voice, and the winces she was having trouble hiding, she'd come out looking for a fight.

I took one of her frail hands in both of mine, and she covered them with her other, giving the top a slight pat. My eyes dropped and my gaze rested beside her on the bed.

"I'm still here," she said after a few moments of silence.

I swallowed the lump of guilt in my throat. "I'm not sure what I would've done if you weren't. I'm sorry, Grams."

"I know you are, but it's not an apology I'm looking for."

I stared up at her firm gaze.

"I want to know when I'm gone that you're taken care of."

All the puzzle pieces suddenly clicked into place.

"How long have you been sick?"

"It doesn't matter. What matters is I want to see my first grandbaby happy and married before I die. I promised myself I'd see that happen, and I have no intention of dying until I do."

"Are you saying if I refuse to, you'll be around forever?"

"No. I'm saying I don't want you to force me to break a promise to myself."

"I don't need to get married to be happy, Grams. I'm already happy and I can take care of myself."

"I don't disagree, and I'd believe that had I not seen the way you lit up around Dr. Chaplin the other night. I'd known it before I'd even seen you together." She lifted a hand to my cheek. "You've never once been curious enough to ask me about a girl, especially a random one you met at a bar. There was a change in you that night. I saw it and I still see it."

"I'm not sure what you saw, but I'm not capable of opening up like that to anyone."

"You are. You have the biggest heart out of everyone in this family. It's a large target, easy to hit, which only makes it more vulnerable. But it's okay to be vulnerable and let that guard down when it's the right one."

"I'm not sure how I feel about you calling me a pussy, Grams."

The yank and twist of my left ear came quick. I laughed despite the slight pain, ducking out of her reach.

"I said no such thing!" She chuckled, despite herself.

There was a knock on the door. "Sounds like a party in here," Dad said, walking into the room.

Tucker followed him, each of them taking their turn to

give Grams a kiss on the cheek. I was relieved at the interruption. The last thing I wanted to do was work Grams up or disappoint her any further.

"Where's Lottie?" I asked, looking over my shoulder, having expected her to follow behind them.

"Looks like we're gonna be adding another member to the family tonight. Hannah just went into labor." Tucker smiled.

"No shit?" My eyes widened.

"Yep. Lottie is with her and Billy, but she'll be by in a bit to see you, Grams. I'm gonna take off to get the kids from Leighton. There's no way she'll want to miss her first niece being born."

"I understand. The babies always need to come first. Don't you worry about it and tell Lottie to take her time. I'm not going anywhere. Hannah needs her right now more than I do. And you boys all need to get yourselves home and get some rest."

"I'm not going anywhere," my dad announced. "You're stuck with me for the rest of the night."

I stood, giving her one last peck on the cheek. "I'm not gonna argue. I've gotta check on Hannah and then drive Devin home. I'll be back by in the morning."

A single gray eyebrow lifted at my mention of Devin. I grinned, giving her a wink before walking out the door, knowing she'd have a million questions for me when I returned.

Devin was seated alone in the waiting room where I'd left

her. "Hey," she said, standing as soon as she saw me. "How is she?"

I pulled her into my arms without a word. She didn't hesitate to wrap herself around me, nuzzling her face into my chest. It felt so damn good. And for the first time since I'd gotten the call, I finally felt myself relax.

After a few minutes, I pulled back to look down at her. "Thank you."

She had no idea what it meant to me to have her there. She'd stayed by my side all night, giving me silent comfort. Being the rock I needed.

She lifted to her toes, giving me a soft kiss on the lips. I knew every nurse and patient in the room was watching us, and that the rumors would be all over town before dawn.

I didn't give a damn.

––––––––

"SHE'S BEAUTIFUL, HANNAH," Devin cooed down at the tiny baby girl bundled in pink and asleep in my arms.

Remy Marie Miller was born less than twenty-four hours ago and already had wrapped those tiny damn fingers around my heart. Maybe I was the pussy Grams said I was.

"She sure is. You sure she's Billy's?" I asked.

All three glared at me. Billy crossed the room immediately, reaching for her.

"Chill out, Miller. It was a joke. You don't have to take her from me." I moved her to the side, holding on tight.

"Give the man his daughter," Devin lectured.

"I will when I'm ready," I shot back. "Besides, I give it a couple weeks and then he'll be begging me to babysit."

"You're crazy if you think I'd ever leave you alone with my daughter."

"Afraid she'll love me more than you?"

"Nope. I figure she'll figure out what a dumbass you are, like every other woman in this town."

Devon and Hannah both snickered at that. Miller was lucky I was holding his baby. "I'm great with kids," I grumbled, not liking one bit that Devin found humor in his comment. "I take care of Lily and Colt all the time."

"He has a point," Hannah jumped in, finally earning her title as my best friend. "As much as I hate to ever give him a compliment, he is a great uncle."

Billy crossed his arms as he looked over at his wife in the hospital bed. She blew him a kiss, making him crack a smile. Accepting defeat, he let me be, with Remy still in my arms.

Devin's phone rang, effectively garnering everyone's attention. She silenced it with a quiet apology, glancing over at Remy.

"She's fine," I assured her.

"I need to take this. I'll meet you outside," she said as she stood. She gave Hannah a hug, promising to stop by later this week after they settled in at home, then left the room.

They'd barely waited for her to clear the doorway before their inquisitive stares were on me. Ignoring them, I looked down at Remy; she'd latched onto one of my fingers with her tiny hand.

"Oh, come on," Hannah complained. "Are you going to make us pull it out of you?"

I knew this was coming as soon as we showed up together at the hospital again. Devin had spent the night at my place. When we left the hospital, I'd taken her to her house, even though it was the last thing I wanted. The moment I saw her hesitation and her searching for the scorpion she'd claimed she saw earlier, I jumped on the opportunity. I told her she was staying with me. And she didn't put up much of an argument.

When morning rolled around, I still hadn't had my fill of her. I insisted she come with me to the hospital, since we both planned to head back to see Grams and Hannah.

"It's none of your business, City."

Hannah huffed, crossing her arms, then gave Billy a silent look.

"No way." He held up his hands, dismissing her imploring stare. "I'm not sticking my nose where it doesn't belong. The man doesn't want to talk about it, then he doesn't want to talk about it."

I took back every bad word I'd ever said about Miller.

"I birthed your child," she tried to manipulate him.

"And I love you for it. You did so good, babe. But that's exactly why I'm not saying a word. I need my job more than ever now."

Smart man.

"He wouldn't fire you."

"He would—"

"I would—"

We spoke in unison. Hannah rolled her eyes.

"Fine. Whatever. You can keep your mouth shut all you want, but it won't keep this town from talking," she warned, as if I needed it. "All the nurses are already whispering about it after how coupled you two looked last night. They even asked me if you were finally officially off the market."

"Let'em talk. They will no matter what I say anyway."

Hannah sighed, relaxing back into the fluffy pillows surrounding her. "Just don't screw this up. We really like Devin, and I want her to continue to hang out with us."

Before I could respond, the room filled with the sounds of gasps and tears of joy from Hannah's parents, who'd just arrived on a last-minute flight from Seattle. Billy's parents followed them in a few seconds later, along with Leighton and Aaron.

The room echoed with their boisterous chatter. I had no idea how Remy was sleeping through it. After passing her off to one of her grandmothers and saying a few quick hellos and goodbyes, I jetted out of there before Hannah could grill me anymore. I knew she'd only let me skirt the subject for so long. I was just glad she'd have her hands full for the foreseeable future.

17

DEVIN

"He'll be fine. I promise," I reassured Mr. Benbrook for the hundredth time.

Being a vet at the zoo had always presented its challenges with the exotic animals, but being a vet in the small town of Billingsley had constantly kept me on my toes. My professionalism had been put to the test on more than one occasion. Until today, I thought nothing would top my appointment last week with Mrs. Hemsworth. She came in with concern for her duck that wasn't swimming. I had no idea how I managed to tell her with a straight face that it was fine because her "duck" was a chicken. She'd blinked up at me through her thick-lensed glasses as if I was the one off my rocker.

"But he's still a male dog?"

"Yes."

"With nipples?"

"Yes."

"And you can't remove them?"

"I don't think that's necessary. It's perfectly normal for him to have them."

"I don't know how it's normal for a male to have nipples."

And that's when I had to bite my tongue to keep from laughing. "You're a male with nipples, are you not?"

He blinked twice before responding. "Yeah. But that's different."

"I assure you, it isn't. Now, unless you have any other questions, Mr. Benbrook, I need to get to my next appointment." The non-existent one. I hated to lie to a client, but it seemed he wasn't leaving until I made some excuse to force him to.

"No"—he shook his head—"no more questions. But I'd like a second opinion. No offense, of course."

I clenched my teeth behind my smile. "No offense taken. I understand. You should always feel free to do so." I gave the large mastiff one more pat on the head, silently apologizing to him for the moron of an owner I was leaving him with. "Okay, boy, time to go," I said to the dog before walking toward the exam room door.

"Is your uncle here?" Mr. Benbrook asked as I opened it for them.

My fist tightened on the knob. He wasn't the first male client who'd questioned my advice simply because I was a young, female vet. "He is. But he's busy with another patient." I plastered on another smile as I turned to face him, waving him through the door with my hand.

His shoulders slumped, and his face fell with disappointment as he led his dog by the leash out into the
reception area. I walked around the counter, handing
Tina his file. As soon as he was gone, leaving the office
empty of clients, I sagged against the counter with a
heavy sigh.

"Hang in there, girl," Tina consoled.

"Is everyone in this town crazy?"

She chuckled as she stood with a stack of patient folders
to file in the cabinet. "Not all. But quite a few. You know,
when he had his dog neutered he asked if we could lock him
in the kennel overnight with a female so he had one last
chance to get his rocks off."

"You're kidding! What did you say?"

She shrugged with her back to me as she opened the
cabinet drawer. "I told him we no longer offered that service."
She peeked over her shoulder at me, a teasing smile on her
face.

I doubled over, clutching my stomach from the laughter
pains. I wiped at the tears that had formed in my eyes as she
took her seat again.

"Speaking of, word on the street is you've gone and
caught yourself Billingsley's most sought-after bachelor."

My smile and good mood quickly disappeared, and I
glanced over at her. "I'm not sure how the two relate, or why
you'd think that was the perfect segue."

"Give me a break." She swatted my arm with the back of
her hand. "I've been dying all week to ask you about it. It's
the best I could do."

"Well, you're going to be disappointed. There's not much to tell," I lied.

I was dying to talk to someone about Wes and me. I hadn't been able to talk to Lottie and the girls, for obvious reasons. And I still wasn't quite comfortable talking to Jenna about him. Plus, I had a good feeling what she'd say. Tina was the only other female friend I had who might have some insight for me, but the warning Wes had delivered about spilling my secrets stuck with me.

Her full lips turned into a pout. "You're telling me you two aren't seeing each other."

Were we?

I had no idea.

We'd spent all last weekend together, mostly in his bed, since that night he'd shown up at my house. But we'd only talked on the phone since then. He'd been working longer hours than normal on the farm, since Billy was at home with Hannah and the baby, and his dad was spending extra time looking after his grams.

As much as I wanted to use his busy schedule as an excuse, deep down I knew it probably wouldn't have mattered. He didn't do relationships. He'd said it time and again. I would only be setting myself up for disappointment if I thought somehow maybe he'd changed his mind.

"No. We aren't," I finally responded. My stomach dropped with disappointment, the same way Tina's expression did.

I stood from the counter with a sigh. It'd been a long week and I was ready to call it a day and start my weekend. "I'm getting out of here."

She nodded, turning back to her computer. As I rounded the counter, the chime for the front door sounded. I looked up at the man coming through it. There was an audible gasp, and it took me a minute to realize it wasn't mine, but Tina's.

She was staring at Wes with a slacked jaw and wide eyes. He gave me one of his gorgeous grins, and I felt my pulse in my throat. I tried to swallow it down, struggling to speak a simple hello. It was absurdly unfair how sexy the man was in a pair of jeans and a basic long-sleeve tee.

My heart thundered as he neared, charging the air with his confident stride.

"Brown eyes. You got a minute?" He stopped, leaving less than a foot between us as he towered over me. The deep tone of his voice saying my pet name sent a shudder down my back.

"Do you have an appointment?" I asked, relaxing my hands on my hips as I tried to stand taller. The last thing I needed was for him to walk up and kiss me in front of Tina after I'd just got done telling her we weren't seeing each other.

"Didn't realize I needed one."

"Well, I'm a busy woman, Mr. Monroe. If you'd like to see me, you should make an appointment."

Tina cleared her throat. "He has an appointment!" she squeaked.

I narrowed my eyes at her as she plucked a pen from her cup and scribbled his name on the appointment calendar on her desk.

"Says right here." She tapped the end of her pen on the

paper. "Sorry, Dr. Chaplin. You must've missed it when you checked earlier."

Wes winked at Tina with an amused smile and she nearly fell out of her chair, blushing like a school girl.

"I was on my way out," I intoned.

"Perfect." Wes stepped closer, his hand tugging at one of my wrists, causing me to stumble forward and bump into his firm chest as I stared up at him. "Because I was looking for more of an after-hours appointment. One off-site."

"A date?" Tina asked in a breathy whisper.

I closed my eyes as the lower parts of my body clenched from the sensations rioting through me, wishing desperately we didn't have an audience. Not that it mattered much at this point. Wes was being anything but subtle.

"Exactly. A date. What do you say, Doc?" He lowered his head, his lips barely brushing my ear. He knew damn well how crazy that drove me. He'd learned it while we were tangled up in his sheets last weekend.

I opened my eyes, my mouth opening and closing as I tried to think of a response.

"I'll grab her purse," Tina chimed in, jumping from her desk, and darting for my office.

"She's helpful." He grinned.

"Yeah. A real go-getter." My voice dripped with sarcasm.

"You should give her a raise."

"She'll be lucky if she has a job tomorrow morning."

His head fell foreword with his deep baritone chuckle, pressing against mine. I bit down on my lip, containing my own giggle. The thrill of being in his arms again after a long week was the best thing I'd ever felt.

Never mind.

I was wrong.

When he finally pressed his lips to mine, *that* was the best thing I'd ever felt.

———

"WHERE ARE WE GOING?" I asked as Wes climbed into his truck beside me. I hadn't had the chance to ask before Tina returned with my purse, shoving it against my chest and pushing us both out the door. He'd followed me to my house, after insisting I change into something more comfortable.

"A concert."

My brow creased as I tried to recall any local bands that might be playing. The only thing I could think of was at Dudley's, but we were heading in the opposite direction. "What concert?"

"Derailed," he answered flippantly, turning on the main highway that ran north and south, leading out of town.

Popping up from the seat, my arm shot out, smacking his bicep in shock. "Shut up! Don't you dare lie to me, slick."

He laughed, his eyes sliding to mine. "Not exactly the response I expected."

With a wide, unblinking stare, my mouth gaped as I tried to process the news. "There's no way you got tickets." I shook my head. "They've been sold out for months."

"I know people," he bragged, his green eyes as smug as his smile.

I tilted my head to the side, pursing my lips.

"Okay. Fine. Timmy knows people," he relented.

I laughed. "I guess Timmy is the one who told you they're my favorite band, too."

He shrugged with a smirk. "Maybe."

I sat back with a giant grin on my face as he passed the city-limit sign. I tried not to read too much into the effort he must've went through to take me on this so-called impromptu date. Noah had never done anything so thoughtful. The few concerts he went to with me, he complained the whole time about the crowds or drink prices.

Wes reached for my hand and I laced our fingers together, delighting in the warmth of his touch as his thumb endlessly caressed my skin the remainder of the drive.

———

EXCITEMENT ENERGIZED my body as we parked. Every tour, Derailed would do a few small concerts in little dive bars across the country, never wanting to forget where they first got their start. I'd tried getting tickets for this one, but they'd sold out in the first thirty minutes. I had no idea how Timmy and Wes had snagged these tickets, and I didn't care. I was just thrilled he'd wanted to take me.

With our hands linked, Wes walked me to the entrance. I was bouncing more than walking at this point, unable to contain the excitement. Wes, on the other hand, was cool and collected as he held the door open for me and passed the tickets to the bouncer.

After grabbing us a few beers, we found an open table near the stage. Wes rested an arm at the back of my chair as he leaned in close. We listened to the opening acts, sharing flirty looks and touches as the loud music reverberated around us. With the heat radiating through me and straight to my center, I'd barely noticed Derailed take the stage. But as soon as the first note played, I was out of my seat, dragging Wes behind me.

Squeezing between a few crazed females, I came to a stop front and center. With his chest pressed to my back, Wes snaked his arms around me. He pressed a sweet kiss against the hot skin on my neck. Tingles broke out inside me as I pulled him tighter around me.

I swayed my hips with the music and he followed the movement as my ass grinded into him. He nipped at my ear for my little tease and I giggled, my head falling against his chest as I watched the band play, humming along with the lyrics.

No matter how things ended between us, I knew this was a night I'd never forget.

————

THE MORNING SUN seeped through a crack in the drawn curtains. Pulling the covers tighter, I squirmed, rubbing my bottom deeper into the crook of Wes' naked body.

I loved the feel of him curled around me as he slept. He squeezed me tighter, groaning into my neck.

"Keep doing that and we'll be going for a repeat of last night." I felt the smile on his lips as he pressed a kiss to my bare shoulder.

I wiggled again and he pinched my waist. Within seconds he had me on my back and my hands pinned above my head as he hovered over me with a sleepy smile.

"You begging for it, Doc?" The scruff on his jaw rubbed against my cheek as he whispered in my ear. He peppered kisses down my throat and across my chest, rendering me speechless.

I moaned as his finger traced the hem of my cotton panties, sliding underneath and dipping inside me. When he added a second, I whimpered, my hips grinding against his hand.

"Shit," he rasped, pulling his hand out and tugging the panties off my hips and down my legs.

Tossing them aside, he hooked his arms under my knees, pulling me closer before diving back in with his tongue. I gasped at the contact, pulling at the short strands of his hair, my hips pushing upward of their own accord.

"Wes," I cried out, barely able to articulate his name as I neared my orgasm.

He didn't relent until I was pulsing and clenching my release. Not giving me any time to recover, he was flipping me over onto all fours, his hands gripping my hips. I pushed back, ready for the force of him plowing into me. When it didn't happen, I glanced over my shoulder at him.

"What are you waiting for?"

He shook his head, his jaw clenched with his tension-filled expression. "I just remembered I'm out of condoms."

My mind raced, my needy body telling me it didn't matter. I'd never not used a condom, and a part of me knew not using one with Wes was dangerous. Not only because of the number of partners he'd had, but also, it was dangerous for my heart. It was a leap of trust I'd never been willing to take. Not even with Noah. Yet, it was one I wanted to take with Wes.

"It's fine. I'm on the pill. And I'm clean. You?"

He nodded, still hesitating. I wiggled my ass at him and he cursed under his breath, digging his fingers deeper into my skin.

"You sure about this?" He hesitated some more, a war waging behind his eyes.

"Wes," I groaned, losing my patience.

Using one hand to fist himself, he lined it up with my entrance. His nostrils flared as he slid inside me, his whole body going rigid. Officially desperate, I pushed back until I felt the fullness of him rooted inside me.

The relief was temporary. He slid out slowly and I whimpered at the loss, but was immediately consoled by the full length of him slamming back inside. He continued to pound into me, his arm curling around my waist as he folded over my back, dotting soft kisses across my skin. I felt the build and release once again, until we were both collapsing onto the mattress in a sated heap.

18

Holding Devin in my arms, I kissed along the back of her bare shoulders. I loved the feel of her warm, damp skin pressed against mine as I remained deep inside her. Giving her one final peck, I slowly pulled out of her wet heat, rolling onto my back to stare at the ceiling.

My mind reeled at what I'd just allowed to happen. I'd never gone raw with any woman. I'd always made sure to wrap it up. If I didn't have a condom, I went without sex. I never felt the need to take such a big risk before. I was breaking all the damn rules for this woman.

Still on her stomach, she twisted to look at me with those big brown-eyes, looking gorgeous with her mussed hair. Her beautiful smile faded as she took me in. "You okay?"

Fuck.

I needed to get control before I hurt her. Rolling to my

side, I lifted to an elbow, kissing her forehead. "I'm good, babe. Just need a shower."

I climbed out of the bed and left the room. As much as I wanted her to join me in the shower, I needed some space to figure out this weird feeling in my chest.

I switched on the water and stepped into the hot spray, letting it pour over the back of my head as I braced myself with both palms flat on the tile wall. The water did nothing to ease the tension in my muscles.

There was a soft knock at the bathroom door. Devin cracked it open, but stayed hidden behind it. "I was going to make some coffee. Is that okay?"

I hated the doubt I heard in her voice. Doubt I'd put there. "Of course, Doc. You don't have to ask."

The door clicked closed without another word from her, and I moved to switch off the water and chase after her. Then I thought better of it. Maybe we both needed a moment.

———

THE SMELL of freshly brewed coffee mingled with the steam-filled air as I opened the bathroom door with a towel wrapped at my waist. Walking into the hall, Devin's completely clothed body caught my eye.

Her brown eyes darkened as she took me in with just one slow blink. With her looking at me that way, the apprehension I'd been feeling earlier was gone. I'd had plenty of women look at me with hungry eyes before, but none of them made me feel as high as she did.

My mouth twitched with a lopsided grin as I prowled toward her, determined to finally take her up against the wall. Her cheeks went pink and she adamantly shook her head. Her eyes were big, round saucers as she backed away from me with a silent warning. She could run all she wanted. I wasn't letting her get away. First, I'd apologize for being a dick earlier, then I'd let her get reacquainted with my di—

"Hey, Uncle Wes." Lily stepped between us, her smile huge. "I brought you cinnamon rolls!" She held up a box from Ida's.

My eyes flicked down to my niece, then back to Devin. "Cinnamon rolls?"

"Yep! Aunt Lottie took me to get them this morning. She said I should bring them to you first thing, so you and Devin didn't starve."

"She did, did she?" I raised a knowing eyebrow. I'd be having a word with Lottie later about using our niece as an informant.

"Uh-huh. You want one?" She shoved the box higher in the air.

I tightened my grip on the towel at my waist.

"Of course, I do. Why don't you take them to the kitchen, and we'll be there in a second."

"Okay. Can I have some milk?"

I nodded. "Just be careful pouring it. Two hands!" I hollered after her as she took off toward the kitchen.

Devin's mouth pursed as she tried to hold back a laugh.

"You think that's funny, do you?" I tugged her into my

arms, tickling her side. She burst out laughing, squirming to free herself from my hold.

"Kinda," she squealed, unashamed as she began to break free. She nipped at my nipple with her teeth and I jumped back away from her, losing my hold. She cackled some more as she backed toward the kitchen, holding her hands up as a shield. "Behave."

"Me?" I mocked offense. "You're the one doing the nipple biting. You're gonna pay for that, brown eyes."

I lunged for her, nearly losing my towel as she darted out of my reach, barely escaping. I caught the towel just before it fell to the floor and she laughed again.

"Go put some clothes on, before you cause your niece to be put through years of therapy," she teased over her shoulder, then disappeared into the kitchen.

————

AFTER PULLING on some jeans and a shirt, I walked back into the kitchen, where Devin and Lily were knee-deep in conversation already. I pulled a mug from the cabinet, making myself a cup of coffee. Leaning against the counter across from the island where they sat, I crossed my ankles and listened as Lily told Devin about a boy at school who had been picking on her lately.

The more she talked, the more I wanted to know who the little shit was, so I could teach him some manners.

"You know, Lily, sometimes boys just don't know how to express their feelings," Devin gently informed her.

"What do you mean?"

"Well sometimes they act one way because they're trying to hide how they truly feel. Most of the time they're just scared or embarrassed for anyone to find out the truth."

I scoffed and they both turned to me.

"What do you think, Uncle Wes?"

"I think the kid needs to watch his back," I grumbled and then closed my mouth when Devin glared at me over Lily's head.

Ignoring my comment, Lily spun back around to look at Devin. "So why does he tease me? What's he hiding?"

"I don't know for sure...has he always teased you?"

"No." She shrugged. "One time, when nobody was looking, he helped me up after I fell on the playground."

I didn't like the sound of that. Devin might be right, but I still wanted to know who this kid was. I planned to keep an even closer eye on him now.

"Maybe he likes you then, but is afraid to tell you."

"Yuck." She scrunched her face.

That's my girl.

Devin laughed as Lily picked up her cinnamon roll and took a bite.

"Yeah, boys can be yuck...but someday you might change your mind about them. And if you do, just remember, even if they might be mean or tease you because they like you, don't allow them to treat you that way. You deserve to be treated with respect, and make sure they know that before you give them the time of day." Devin's eyes locked with mine as she delivered her last bit of advice.

I swallowed hard, then shoved a hand deep into my pocket as I took a sip, hiding behind my coffee mug. I'd fucked up earlier and I knew that. She'd given me a part of her that I hoped to hell she'd never given anyone else. But instead of cherishing her afterward, I pushed her away because of my own fears.

"Are you a midnight romp?" Lily asked out of nowhere as she took another bite, her legs swinging innocently on the bar stool.

I choked on my coffee, coughing, and covering my mouth with my arm before I sprayed it all over the floor.

Devin's eyes widened as she stumbled for a response. "Oh, uh...I think that's a great question for your Uncle Wes." She patted Lily's hand, and stood from her seat. Lily spun around once again and I froze. Her little expectant eyes were glued to me as I watched Devin retreat out of the kitchen.

Shit.

———

ONCE I'D EFFECTIVELY DISTRACTED LILY from her question and she finally left, I searched my house for Devin. The panic started to build when I couldn't find her. Then I remembered, she didn't have a car to get home. She couldn't have gotten far on foot.

I pulled on my boots and snatched my keys and phone off the entry table as I charged out the front door. I was already dialing Tucker, in case she decided to walk to their place, when I saw her dark hair whipping in the breeze from the corner of my eye. I skidded to a stop.

She was standing in the middle of the field with her arms crossed over her body as she tried to warm herself. She looked angelic in the morning sun as she watched a few of our horses in the distance. My shoulders relaxed as I hit end and slid the phone and keys into my pocket.

Stopping behind her, I wrapped her in my arms. She didn't lean into me like I'd hoped. She didn't pull away either. I prayed that was a good sign.

"I'm sorry," I spoke low and quiet into her neck, dropping a kiss on it.

She let out a heavy exhale and then spun in my arms to face me. Her breasts lifted with her arms as she hugged herself tighter, revealing the slightest bit of cleavage. When my cock pulsed alive, I fought the urge to press into her with my hips. This wasn't the time.

"What are we doing here, Wes?" she whispered at my chest.

I tucked my hand under her chin, lifting her gaze to mine. I studied her for a moment before answering. There was a sharp shooting pain in my chest when I saw the hurt, the barricade she was quickly putting up. She was taking a step back, withdrawing from whatever *this* was.

"I don't know," I confessed. "All I know is I like spending time with you. And I'm not ready for it to end."

"Yet," she snapped. "You're not ready for it to end, *yet*."

"I don't know what you want from me, Devin. I'm trying

to be honest with you here. If this isn't what you want, then you need to tell me."

"I don't know what I want!" She shoved off me, stomping away a few feet before whipping back around. "I like you Wes!" Her arms flailed at her sides in frustration. "I'm not good at this casual stuff. I'm trying to be, because I like being with you, but it's hard for me."

I rubbed my hand down my face and over the back of my neck as I looked at the ground. This shit was too much. The last thing I wanted to do was hurt her, but I couldn't seem to let her go.

"Do we have to put a label on it? Is that what you need?" I asked.

"No. It's fine. Just forget I even said anything. Can you take me home?"

"Devin—"

"It's fine, slick. We're good. I'm exhausted and just need to go home." She turned to walk away from me once again.

I wasn't having it. There was no way in hell I was leaving things unsettled between us. I latched on to her wrist, pulling her to a stop and back into my arms.

"We aren't done here, brown eyes." I cupped her face, forcing her to look at me. "I know I screwed up earlier. I'm sorry. What happened between us this morning was new for me. Everything that's happening between us is new to me, so I'm gonna need you to cut me some slack. I'm trying here, Doc." I tucked her hair behind her ear, dropping my eyes to the lips I wanted to kiss so damn bad. "Give me a chance."

She closed her eyes, taking a deep breath through her nose.

My stomach dropped. Rejection wasn't something I was used to. I wasn't sure I could handle it, especially from her.

"Okay," she breathed, her eyes flicking open. "But I'm only agreeing because I'm not ready to be alone in that house again with the scorpion."

There was fire in her eyes as she teased me, and I felt a heavy weight lift from my chest.

"Just admit it, Doc. You made that shit up so you could see the 'scorpion' in my pants."

She smacked my chest playfully. I tucked her closer to me, pressing my mouth against hers, prodding at the seam of her lips until she let me in. She squealed and grinned against my mouth when I lifted her into my arms. As I walked us back inside the house, I swore I'd never hurt her like that again. It was a risky promise to make. But when it came to her, I was never in my right mind.

———

"You're smiling a lot lately."

"I've always smiled a lot." I kissed Grams' cheek while she sat in her recliner, holding Colton, then took a seat on the couch with Remy plastered against my chest.

"Yeah. But this is a different smile. It's lighter."

"Grams," I warned, lightly rubbing Remy's back as she began to doze off.

"All right. I'm just pointing out you seem much happier these days."

I was. I was so fucking ecstatic every day that I couldn't help the dopey smile on my face. Today was the first day I hadn't seen Devin in weeks. I invited her to have Thanksgiving with us, but she said she needed to be with her family at their lake house. She hadn't seen her parents or Jenna since leaving Austin a few months ago.

It sucked being away from her, but was probably for the best. With things going so well between us, I didn't want anything or anyone messing it up.

Lily ran into the living room with Tucker, Aaron, and Billy behind her. She stopped in front of me, bouncing on the balls of her feet. "You wanna come play with us?"

I looked over at the guys for more information. "We're gonna toss the ball around until dinner's ready." Tucker held up the football in his hand.

My eyes went to Remy, who was now fast asleep. I'd volunteered to hold her while Hannah attempted to help Lottie and Leighton prepare Thanksgiving dinner. They'd taken over Grams' kitchen and pushed her out. She wasn't all too happy about it, but she'd given up arguing. I wasn't sure if she was more upset about everyone still coddling her after the heart attack, or the fact that she had to pass over some of her favorite recipes so they could make them.

"I got her. Hand her over," my dad ordered as he walked into the room. I wasn't surprised by his demand. The old man seemed to be going soft these days.

He took her from me, then took my seat on the couch as I

vacated it. Lily had already squealed and ran out the door, her ponytail swishing behind her.

We split up into teams for a game of tag football: Billy and Aaron against Lily and me. Tucker was the designated quarterback for both teams. We played for about an hour before Lottie came out onto the porch, hollering for us to come in and wash up.

"I half expected Devin to be joining us today." Tucker walked beside me as the other two raced Lily to the porch.

I shrugged, tossing the ball up in the air and catching it. "She has her own family."

"Yeah. But you two have been spending a lot of time together. Plus, she's been here every Sunday dinner. You getting serious about this one?"

"Do I ever?"

He clapped my back. "I get it, man. I didn't like it when you tried to give me advice either. But I'm not too proud to admit I'm glad you pushed me when you did. Things might have turned out a whole lot different if you hadn't." His eyes went to Lottie, who was laughing and joking with the others on the front porch. "Letting go of the past and showing up at her house that night was the best decision I ever made."

"You're welcome." I puffed out my chest with a smug grin, tossing the ball up one more time.

He intercepted it, drawing my attention to him. "You can't change the past, man, but you can change your future. I've never had to ask you why you choose not to get close to anyone, because I get it. Trust me, man. *I get it.* We went through the same losses. And I was on the same page as you for years until Lottie showed back up in my life. You hear what I'm saying?"

I pushed my hands in my pockets, looking away from him and across the field at the setting sun. I hated that he was fucking right. "I hear you."

"Good." He squeezed my shoulder, then jogged a few steps forward before turning and throwing the football up in the air.

I caught it. He winked at me, and I realized how annoying that was. He took the steps two at a time, pulling Lottie into his arms, and dipping her for a kiss. She squealed and giggled as she clung to his neck, kissing him back.

My heart clenched. I rubbed at it when I realized how badly I wanted that to be Devin and me, right now.

————

PULLING THE DOOR OPEN, I strolled into Ida's with one thing on my mind.

Devin.

She'd become addicted to cinnamon rolls. I'd become addicted to tasting them on her lips. After four days of being apart over the holidays, I couldn't wait to see her. I'd come into town to run a few errands and decided I'd pop in and see my woman before heading back to the farm.

My woman.

I'd never claimed any girl as mine before. We still hadn't officially labeled what was happening between us, but I was finally ready to. I'd spent the last few nights alone in my bed with nothing to do but think. I wanted more than friends with benefits. I wanted everything with Devin. And I planned to tell her that today.

"Keep the change." I smiled and winked out of habit at the young cashier, passing her my money.

She blushed, sliding the box of cinnamon rolls and coffee across the counter. "Thanks, Mr. Monroe."

I picked them up, not wasting another minute. I loved making women smile, but right now, there was only one woman's smile I wanted to see.

"We'll see you soon, Otis." I bent at the waist, giving the black lab a good scratch behind his ear. I waved bye to his human family as they walked out the door, dropping his file on the counter by Tina.

"I'm gonna pop over to Ida's for a coffee. Do you want anything?"

"No, thank you," she answered, keeping her eyes focused on where she was writing down some notes. "Oh!" She glanced up as I started to walk away. "Before I forget. You have a visitor. A very charming and handsome one who insisted on waiting for you in your office." The corners of her lips curved upward, and her eyebrows wagged.

I laughed. No matter how many times she asked and I denied it, we both knew Tina was aware of the time I spent with Wes. It was now an ongoing joke between us. I still had no idea what we were, but after things being great between us over the last month, I wasn't pushing to label it anymore.

I was happy. And for now, that was all that mattered. I opened my door, ready to greet Wes with a big, wet kiss, only to stop short in the opening.

"Noah," I gasped, covering my rolling stomach with my hand.

"Hey, baby." He stood from where he'd been leaning against my desk and strode toward me with a cocky smile. I flinched as his hands wrapped around my arms, pulling me to him. I turned my head, forcing his lips to meet my cheek. "I missed you."

I shrugged out of his hold, taking a step back. "What are you doing here?"

"I told you. I missed you. And we need to talk about everything."

"There's nothing I want to talk to you about," I scowled. "I figured I'd made that clear when I refused to accept your calls."

"You just needed time to cool off, Dev. I get it. But it's been months now. I thought we could talk and work things out."

"You need to leave, Noah."

"Come on, baby. Don't be like that. I came all this way to see you and I'm not leaving until we've talked."

"Fine. Say what you need to say and then leave."

He smiled, taking a step forward. I immediately regretted

my decision. Once again, I felt weak in his presence. Not because I wanted to be with him, but because he'd always made me feel inferior, or less than worthy.

"I'm gonna make this right, baby. I made a mistake. *She* was a mistake. When I realized how much I loved you, I freaked out and tried to deny my feelings by sleeping with her. But I'm not scared anymore. I know we belong together and that's why"—he lowered to one knee, taking a ring from his pocket and grabbing my left hand before I knew what was happening—"I want you to marry me, Devin. Forgive me. Make an honest man out of me."

My jaw slacked open as I stared down at the ring he was trying to slide onto my finger. I pressed my free hand to my forehead, feeling lightheaded and dizzy. There was no way this was happening right now. *How* could this be happening right now? For years, all I ever wanted was for this man to propose. Now that it was happening, I felt sick.

Before I could say or do anything to stop him, there was a small commotion at my door. I turned to see Wes seething in the opening, a box of cinnamon rolls and a coffee cup spilling over at his feet.

It all happened so fast, my brain barely registered what was going on. My eyes widened as I watched him look between Noah and me, our hands still connected.

"Wes!" I cried out as he spun to leave.

I tugged my hand from Noah's and ran after him. He was already at his truck when I finally caught him. Pulling at his arm, I grappled to stop him. "Wes, please! Just wait. Let me explain."

He twisted out of my grasp, stepping away from me. "Explain what, Devin? That you're suddenly engaged?"

"It's not what you think. Things are complicated. We have history." *Damn it!* I instantly regretted how that sounded. But the words were out. I reached for him again, hoping somehow my touch would calm us both. "That's not what I mean."

He flinched away, ignoring my attempt at taking it all back. "And what about us? Whatever he's promising you, it's not gonna be permanent. He's not gonna change, Devin."

His words stung, and it had nothing to do with Noah.

"And you are?" I challenged, pissed that he had the nerve to point fingers when he wasn't even willing to say we were in a relationship.

"No." He shook his head, his face stern. Every part of him went rigid with his dark eyes. "The fact that I've fallen in love with you and wish by some stroke of luck you'd be mine, will never change. I'm not saying that I'm perfect. God and everyone knows, I'm not. But I was willing to give us a shot." He yanked his truck door open and climbed inside.

"Wes! Wait! You can't just say something like that to me and then leave."

"Watch me," he barked, slamming his door shut.

Standing shell-shocked, I watched him fire up his truck and peel off. I wiped the tears that had slid down my cheek and spun back around, ignoring all the stares aimed my direction from the townsfolk passing by on the sidewalk.

I jerked the door to the clinic open, stomping through.

Tina was on her feet with worry and remorse all over her face.

I held up my hand as she began to speak, all my attention focused on the man now coming out of my office. "Get out!" I pointed at the front door.

"Dev—"

"No! I said get out, Noah!" I ripped the ring from my finger, chucking it at him. He fumbled a little before catching it.

"You don't mean that," he pleaded.

"I do. And don't ever come back. Stop calling me. Just leave me the hell alone!"

"We belong together, baby." He moved toward me and my uncle came out of nowhere, slipping between us.

"You heard her, boy. Get the hell out of my office before I make you."

Noah clenched his fists at his sides as he glared at my uncle and then me. I stood taller, my chin in the air, feeling stronger than ever, despite the tears streaming down my red cheeks.

"Fine." He shoved past my uncle, stopping at my side. "Your loss, sweetheart. You don't deserve this."

"You're right. I deserve better."

The cocky attitude he wore like a badge of honor fell. With one final glance, he disappeared out the front door.

Uncle Robert pulled me to his chest and I lost it. There was no stopping the tears and regret now. Tina ran around the counter, wrapping her arms around me from behind, sandwiching me between them.

"I'm so sorry, Devin. I had no idea that was Noah. He just said he was an old friend from Austin. I would have kicked him out had I known."

I slid away from them both, turning to look at Tina as I wiped the tears. "It's fine, Tina. It's not your fault."

We gave each other another hug.

"I need you to reschedule my appointments for the rest of the day."

"Of course, not a problem." She nodded.

"You can fill any openings I have for the day," Uncle Robert directed. He squeezed my shoulder as he looked over at me with a gleam in his eye. "Go get'em."

I nodded, hugged my uncle, and after grabbing my things, charged out the front door on a mission.

———

THE WHEELS of my car slid on the gravel as I slammed on the brakes next to Wes' parked truck. I was out of my car and scanning the area as fast as I could, finding no sign of him.

My eyes landed on Billy walking out of the barn, wiping his hands on an old rag.

"Billy!"

He looked up, his face twisting in confusion as he took me in, racing toward him. "Doc. What are you doing here? What's going on?"

"Wes," I breathed, trying to suck in as much oxygen as I could. "Where is he?"

He shook his head. "Not sure. Haven't seen him." He

looked past me at Wes' truck, then met my gaze again. "He may be out on the tractor."

"Can you take me to him?"

"Sure. Everything okay?"

I shook my head. "I just need to talk to him."

"Okay. Jump in." He waved a hand toward his own truck.

I ran to the passenger door, hurriedly sliding into the seat. I was thankful Billy didn't waste any time doing the same.

The ride was silent. My mind was going a hundred miles per hour as I tried to come up with what I was going to say to Wes when I saw him.

Billy pulled to the side of the dirt road, shifting into park then leaning against the steering wheel as he pointed out the window toward a tractor. "That's him. Stay here. I'll get his attention." He opened his door.

I nodded, even though the last thing I wanted to do was sit tight with anxious energy coursing through me. But I figured having Billy signal him over was better than me. If I did, there was a good chance he'd just keep on going.

Billy waded through the field, pulling off his cap and waving it in the air to flag Wes down. The tractor stopped in the distance. The roar of the engine died. Wes climbed down from the tractor, walking toward Billy, and my heart about stopped at the sight of him.

Flinging the door open, I jumped down from the seat. I slammed it shut just as both of their heads whipped around to look at me.

All the nerves I'd felt earlier doubled when I saw the pissed-off look on his face. He wasn't happy to see me. They exchanged a few words. Then Billy slapped his shoulder, leaving Wes standing in the field as he strolled back to me.

"Good luck, Doc," he said as he neared. "You want me to wait?"

I swallowed the hard lump in my throat. "Probably a good idea." I was no longer confident things were going to turn out as well as I'd hoped.

Billy nodded, then got back in his truck, leaving me and Wes in a faceoff. Inhaling a deep breath, I took the first step to him. His hands were on his hips, his cap on backward, making it impossible for me to miss the anger in his eyes as I approached.

"Hey," I choked out the word.

"What are you doing here, Devin?" His chest lifted as he crossed his arms over it with a stone-faced expression.

"I need to explain what happened back there. And we need to talk about what you said to me."

"I've said all I need to say."

"Okay. Fine. Then I'll do all the talking." I huffed, pushing some wind-blown strands of hair from my face. "What you saw was a misunderstanding. I'm not getting married. At least, not any time soon and not to Noah. Ever. I was seconds away from telling him just that when you walked in. He's my ex. The one who hurt me. We'd been together for four years when I walked in on him screwing one of his co-workers.

"Things were over between us as soon as I saw them. They were probably over long before that. I was just having trouble admitting that to myself. He'd always had this weird power over me that made me feel weak. But not anymore. I'm stronger. I know what I'm worth and it's taken me a long time to realize I deserve more. And I'm not going to take less than I deserve any longer. Not even from you."

He looked away from me, his jaw ticking.

"These last few months together have been some of the best of my life. And I want to see where things go with us, Wes. But if you're gonna take the first chance you get to cut and run, then I'm not gonna hold you down. If space is what you need, if a casual fuck is what you want, then fine. But it won't be with me. I can't keep pretending I don't want more with you, because despite my best efforts, I've fallen too."

I waited for him to meet my eyes. Waited for him to say something. Anything. When he didn't, I felt the crack in my heart. Protecting what was left of it, and hanging on to my pride, I turned and walked away without another word. I wasn't going to beg and plead with him. He knew where I stood. It was his decision now.

———

"WHO WANTS EGGNOG?" my mother asked, a jubilant smile on her face as she walked in with a bottle of whiskey in her hand.

"Oh! Me!" Jenna raised her hand, plopping down on the couch beside me in her Christmas onesie. Everyone in my family was wearing an identical one, and we all looked equally ridiculous.

"Devin?" My mom directed her eyes to me. I hadn't been paying attention to them. I'd been in a daze for what felt like months now.

With their stares both on me, I sighed. "Sure. Why not," I added, dryly. "Minus the eggnog."

Mom narrowed her eyes in disapproval before leaving the room again to make our drinks.

Jenna bumped my shoulder. "Can you at least pretend to be in a good mood? Your mom is worried about you. We all are."

"I'll try."

She plucked a hand from my lap, tugging me to my feet.

"Where are we going?"

"To talk," she declared over her shoulder as she dragged me up the stairs and into her childhood bedroom.

She pushed me toward her twin bed to sit, then flung open her closet doors. Lifting to her toes, she dug through the boxes on the top shelf. Finally finding what she was looking for, she pulled down an old tattered shoe box and faced me.

I arched an eyebrow.

She grinned, flipping the lid off the top and pulling out a half-full bottle of cheap tequila.

"Do I want to know how old that is?"

"Does it matter?" She walked to the bed with the bottle, dropping the box on the floor.

"Nope. Hand it over." I reached out my hand.

She passed it to me. I twisted off the cap and took a drink. I coughed as I pulled it away. "That shit is terrible."

The bed dipped as she crawled onto it beside me. "You want me to throw it out?"

"No." I shook my head, passing it to her as we both settled back against her headboard with our legs outstretched in front of us.

"So, what happened?" she asked after a few silent shots between us, all of them tasting just as terrible as the first.

"Noah happened."

She let out an aggravated sigh. "I know that part. Dad filled me in. I want to know what happened when you took off after Wes."

"Nothing."

"Dee," she whined.

"Really. Nothing. I found him on his farm. Laid everything out there for him and he said *nothing*."

It'd been weeks since that day and I hadn't seen or heard from Wes, which only meant he was taking special care to avoid me in our small town. Every time my phone rang, someone knocked on my door, or came into the office unexpectedly, I hoped it would be him. But every time I was left with nothing but disappointment.

She slid an arm around my shoulders. We leaned into each other, the sides of our heads pressing together. "I'm sorry."

"You can say you told me so."

"I'd never do that... Besides, from what I heard, I was wrong. You got to him, Dee."

"Don't tell me that. You'll just give me hope. And I can't handle it. I need to move on."

She hugged me tighter to her side as I fought back the welling tears.

"It's all gonna work out however it's supposed to. You'll see."

I nodded. There was a light knock on the jamb as Jenna's husband, Brad, popped his head in.

"Sorry to interrupt girl-talk, but just letting you know I'm gonna run to the store. Apparently, we are out of flour and the kids are demanding homemade sugar cookies for Santa."

We both lifted our heads, pulling apart. "I can go, if you want," I offered. I was dying to get out of the house. I loved my family, but I could use some alone time.

"Actually, I was already planning a trip. I need a few things from the store," Jenna said, jumping forward. She squeezed my hand and slid off the bed. She whispered something in Brad's ear. He smiled and then gave her a kiss before she disappeared.

"What was that about?" I asked Brad.

He pulled his fingers across his mouth, silently zipping his lips. I tossed a pillow at him and he ducked with a laugh. "You know Jenna. What do you think that was about?"

My face paled as it dawned on me. "Tell me she's not going where I think she is."

He shrugged with a smile, crossing his arms. I jumped from the bed, ready to charge after her. He blocked the doorway, barricading me in the room with his body.

"Brad, this isn't funny."

"Didn't say it was. But I'm also not breaking a promise to my wife."

I pinned my hands on my hips, trying my best to intimidate him. It didn't work. "You two suck," I pouted.

"You'll get over it."

20

I opened my front door with a scowl on my face. I was in no mood for company. Even though it was Christmas Eve, I was avoiding my family, preferring to be alone and away from their nagging and disappointed stares.

"What are you doing here?"

Roger glanced at the nearly empty whiskey bottle in my hand. "Your dad called. Said there was a belligerent drunk hanging out on his property."

I scoffed and turned, leaving the door wide open as I walked away. He closed it behind him, following me into the kitchen and taking a seat at the bar.

I abandoned the bottle on the counter. It wasn't doing its job anyway of ridding the memories of Devin from my mind. I opened my fridge, grabbed two beers, and passed him one. The crack of the aluminum cans echoed off the walls of the silent room.

He took a drink, then sighed with appreciation before setting the can on the counter. "So, you and the Doc broke up," he announced after a few moments.

"You can't break up if you were never together."

"Yeah." He rolled his eyes like a teenage girl. "Keep telling yourself that. Seems to be doing a lot of good."

"You come here to lecture me?" I griped, leaning my back against the counter, taking a big swallow of the weak beer.

"Nope. We both know that shit doesn't work when it comes to you. Besides, figure you already got a line of people waiting to do just that."

"Then what are you doing here?"

"I needed a free beer."

"You get those at Dudley's all the time."

"It's Christmas Eve. Timmy closed early for once." He pressed the can to his mouth, taking another sip.

I gave him the side-eye.

"Fine. I'm here to lecture you. Sue me. It's my right as your friend. In all the years I've known you, which is a long fucking time, I've never once seen you this tore up over a woman. Not even Jenna."

"It's over."

"Word around town is that's your choice. So, tell me why you're sitting here, drowning in a bottle of whiskey, instead of curled up with her by a cozy fucking fire, snuggled under a blanket, sipping on cocoa."

"That's a pretty picture you just painted."

"Yeah, I'm a real Van Gogh. Stop deflecting."

I dragged a palm over the scruff I hadn't bothered to

shave in days. There was another knock at my front door. My brow creased as I looked that direction. "Who is that?"

"Hell if I know. It's your house."

I exhaled, slamming my can on the counter. I muttered a line of curses as I stomped to the door and swung it open. I stilled when I saw the woman standing in my porch light.

"Hey, stranger," her voice trembled slightly with a nervous smile as she tucked her dark hair behind her ear.

It took me a few seconds to realize she wasn't just my imagination. "Cricket," I responded, scanning her from head to toe. "Nice pajamas."

She laughed, and something inside me stirred.

Roger cleared his throat from behind me. I stepped to the side, twisting to look at him.

"I'm gonna take off." He slid past me, giving me a clap on the shoulder. "Nice to see ya, Jenna. You look good."

She did a mock curtsy in her ridiculous pajamas as she grinned. "Thanks, Roger. I didn't mean to run you off."

"No, worries. I was on my way out anyway." Taking the steps down from my porch, he looked over his shoulder at me with a worried expression I didn't understand.

What the hell did he think was gonna happen?

I watched him leave, trying to figure out how my night had turned out this crappy, and why everyone felt the need to drop by unexpectedly. I scanned the fields, wondering if they were all hiding in them, waiting for their turn to bombard me with their stupid words of wisdom.

"Can I come in?" Jenna asked, drawing my attention back

to her. She was pulling the edges of her coat snug across her chest.

"Yeah." I nodded, stepping aside.

She walked past me, stopping just inside the entry. Her eyes traveled through the room as mine traveled over her. She looked good. She looked happy. Even in those silly pajamas.

She slid out of her jacket, handing it over to me. I took it and hung it up on the coat rack. She clasped her hands in front of her, looking at me expectantly.

I cleared my throat, nervous about being alone with her. It was a weird feeling, one I couldn't quite put my finger on. I'd say it was guilt, but as far as I was concerned, I had nothing to feel guilty about. "You wanna drink?"

"No. I'm driving and already had a few shots of tequila before getting the nerve to come over here."

Tequila.

I couldn't even hear the word without thinking of Devin. If I had to take a guess, they were likely doing those shots together, and that was the reason for Jenna's visit.

I tucked my hands in my pockets, ducking my head. It pissed me off to think about Devin sitting somewhere taking shots of tequila because of me. I was pissed at how things ended. Pissed at the world for its unfairness. Pissed at myself for a million reasons I didn't want to go into.

"She loves you, Wes."

My head snapped up at the sound of her words. Four words and she had my undivided attention. I wanted to know everything Devin might have told her behind closed doors.

But I wouldn't ask. Because the shit between us was over. Finished. Done.

Her body softened, her eyes full of the same sadness and disappointment I'd seen in them when I left her behind years ago. "You love her, too. I can see it. Even after all these years, I can still see the real you."

"Don't Jenna." I dug my fingers into my palms.

"Why Wes? Why can't you just open up?"

"Jenna," I warned again, but she just kept pushing.

"She's not gonna wait forever for you to stop being a jackass."

"This is none of your business."

"It is!" She stepped into my space, poking a pointed finger into my chest, causing me to take a small step back. "She's my cousin! My best friend! And so were you at one point in our lives until you pushed me away!"

"You were already gone!" I roared, my breath heaving with every excruciating heartbeat I was forced to feel. Her words were like weights, dragging me down to the bottom of the ocean.

"No, Wes. I was right there. I've always been there for you. You just refused to ever fully open up to me. You couldn't even tell me how you felt about me all those years ago."

"Is that what this is about? Are you jealous? Mad that I slept with your cousin and not you?" I smarted off.

"Fuck you, Wes," she gritted through her teeth.

"No, thanks," I sneered, taking another step back, folding my arms across my chest. "I may be a prick, but I draw the line at married women."

"I don't know why I even bothered," she huffed, brushing past me and yanking her jacket from the hook. She whipped back around to face me as she struggled into it. "I thought if I talked to you, you'd come to your senses and realize you were about to let a great woman slip away. I guess I was hoping you'd changed." She reached for the doorknob.

"Shit," I cursed, pulling at my neck. Even with the alcohol muddling my brain, I knew I couldn't let her leave like this. "Cricket, wait!" I grabbed her arm, stopping her. "I'm sorry. I didn't mean all that. I'm a dick. We both know that." And I'd probably had way too much to drink, not that I'd be using that as an excuse.

She yanked her arm away, still glaring at me.

"Please." I looked away, blowing out a breath. "Stay... I could use the company."

She crossed her arms, her eyes narrowing with suspicion. "I won't sleep with you."

I felt an unexpected laugh bubble up, trying to burst from my mouth, thinking back to the night I first met Devin and how alike they were, yet so different.

"I wouldn't dream of sleeping with you either, not just because you're married...but because I'm in love with your cousin." I stared back at her.

She smiled, her posture relaxing. "I knew it. Now we just have to figure out how you're gonna get her back."

The little pussy in my chest jumped at that. "You think she'll take me back?"

"With my help, yeah. But you'll have to do a lot of groveling. To both of us, after your douchebag comment earlier."

For the first time in what had to be weeks, my lips curled up in a genuine smile. "It's good to see you, Cricket."

"You too, Wes. I missed you."

"Same." I hugged her to me.

Her little arms snaked around me, giving me a tight squeeze before they fell away. "All right, enough of that." She pushed from me, walking into my living room and tossing her coat aside. "We've got our work cut out for us."

21

DEVIN

My bed bounced. Then a few sweet giggles erupted beside me. "Wake up, Devin! Santa came!"

I groaned, rolling onto my stomach, covering my head with my pillow at the sounds of Jenna's girls' laughter. I wasn't feeling so great after finishing off the bottle of shit tequila Jenna had left me alone with. I'd planned to drive home to stay at my own place, but thought better of it when the buzz from the tequila kicked in.

One of their tiny hands prodded me in the ribs.

"Give me five more minutes," I moaned.

"Momma says we can't open the presents until everyone is up."

She would. It was likely a ploy just to torture me some more. She'd been like Fort Knox when she returned home late last night. When asked what took so long for her to get flour, she'd claimed they were out at the local supermarket and she had to drive to the next town over to get some. I knew something was up the moment I cornered her and asked her point blank if she'd gone to see Wes. She avoided my eyes while denying it.

That was fine. I knew the truth. It just made me wonder what had been said between the two of them, and if she was lying to spare my feelings. I dropped it after that, deciding I didn't want to know. I was more determined than ever to move past the heartbreak he'd left me with.

"Pleaaasssse," they begged in unison. "Wake up!"

I twisted to my back, tossing the pillow from my head. "Fine. But you each owe me your share of Christmas cookies in payment."

They giggled and then jumped off my bed, running out of the guest bedroom, screaming, "She's up! Can we open now?"

With one more stretch and another groan, I pulled myself out of my bed. I padded across the wood floors of my aunt and uncle's house to their guest bathroom. After struggling with the stupid onesie, I went to the bathroom, washed my face, and brushed my teeth.

The house smelled of fresh coffee and sweet baked goods as I made my way downstairs, where all the rambunctious voices of my family were.

I took a seat on the couch next to my mother, who was watching the girls sift through all the presents, looking for the ones that belonged to them. She patted my leg and I rested my head on her shoulder.

"Merry Christmas, honey."

"Merry Christmas, Mom." I forced a smile. Even though I felt anything but merry, I put on a happy face for her. I didn't want to be the Scrooge that ruined my family's Christmas.

Jenna sat on the other side of me, handing me a cup of coffee. "Peace offering."

"Thank you," I relented, taking it from her. I couldn't stay mad at her anyway. Plus, the coffee smelled freaking awesome.

"You're welcome." She smiled, lightly bumping my shoulder.

The rest of the family filed in soon after. My dad kissed my mom, then the back of my head before taking his own seat across the room. The sounds of excited voices and laughing took over as we spent the rest of the morning opening gifts around the Christmas tree.

———

AFTER BREAKFAST, I stuffed the ugly onesie back in my bag and zipped it closed. Slipping my arms through the sleeves of my flannel shirt, I did a final scan of the room to make sure I had everything.

"Leaving so soon?" Jenna's voice came from behind me.

"Yeah. I'm sorry." I glanced at her. "I'm kind of exhausted and need some quiet time. I'll come back before you guys leave tomorrow."

She walked deeper into the room, taking a seat on the bed. "I get it. Sometimes, I wish I could slip away and hide from everyone, too. What I'd give for a few moments of peace and quiet these days."

"You're welcome to come with me. We can share a bottle of wine and binge on Netflix."

"Ugh. Sounds like heaven. Don't tempt me."

I chuckled, picking up my bag and resting the strap on my shoulder. "Last chance."

"Nah, you go ahead. I don't think Brad will forgive me if I disappear on him two days in a row, leaving him alone with the kids and in-laws."

She stood from the bed, giving me a hug. I squeezed her tight, missing her already.

"Oh, good. You're still here," Uncle Robert interrupted with a relieved sigh as he stopped outside the room. "There was a message on the emergency line for the clinic."

"Is everything okay?" I asked.

He shook his head, glancing over at Jenna and then back to me. "No. I could use your help on this one. You mind riding with me?"

"Of course not. What's going on?"

"It's a couple horses outside of town."

"Let me get my kit. I'll meet you at the car," I confirmed without hesitation, already rushing out the door.

———

UNCLE ROBERT HAD little information about the situation for me as we drove. It was abnormal for him, but I chalked it up to a panicked client not giving him much in the voicemail.

It wasn't until we slowed at the entrance to the Monroe farm that I realized the expression on his face, the one I'd interpreted as concern for the animals, was guilt, and likely concern for his own wellbeing.

"What are we doing here?" I turned on him.

"Don't be mad at me, kiddo. This wasn't my idea."

"But you're taking part in it anyway."

He cringed at my tone. "I'm sorry. The women in this family can be very convincing...and scary." He eyed me, leaning away and closer to the driver's door.

"Is this even really an emergency?"

"Depends who you're asking." He slowed the car outside the massive horse barn. He shifted it into park before turning to face me. "Do you hate me?"

"No. Not if you turn this car around and take me home, now."

He gave me a weak smile, his eyes full of remorse. "No can do. I love you, but I also love golf. And I've been promised a weekend of it if I did this."

"You're selling me out for golf!" I gawked.

"Yep," he declared, the remorse long gone.

I blew out my breath in annoyance as I latched on to the handle. "Fine. Let's get this over with."

We walked toward the barn and around a large trailer hitched to a truck I didn't recognize. I expected for Wes to be the person to greet us. Instead, it was Tucker walking up, with Lily bouncing with anticipation beside him. I looked back at the trailer, where I heard a horse kicking around inside, suddenly remembering the Christmas surprise Lily was getting today.

"Devin!" she squealed, running full speed and wrapping me in a hug at my waist. "Did you come to see my horse?"

Bending at the knees, I lowered, taking her little hand in mine. "I sure did." As much as it would annoy me, I truly hoped this was a trick and nothing was wrong with her horse.

Uncle Robert and Tucker exchanged a quick greeting and handshake before Tucker was playfully tugging at Lily's ponytail. "You ready to see her, Lily-pad?"

"Yep!" Her cheeks were pink from the cold wind hitting them as she grinned, her eyes full of joyous excitement.

The trailer door slowly swung open as Clark Thomas led the filly we'd visited months ago out of the trailer. She had a big red bow at her neck and a new tan saddle with pink stitching already on her back.

Lily jerked Tucker forward as she took off. He was the only thing weighing her down and keeping her from running in a full-on sprint toward her new horse.

I watched as Tucker helped her into the saddle. Her whole body radiated a contagious joy. I'd been so focused on the heartfelt moment, I hadn't noticed the others joining us from inside the house, not until I felt Wes pressing close behind me.

His hand landed at the small of my back as he leaned down, his low voice meeting my ear. "Can I show you something?"

My stomach stirred, taking flight as soon as his breath had brushed against my cheek. Without looking at him, I nodded, unable to form words, too focused on the heat of his touch and the tenderness of it as he rubbed his thumb lightly over my back.

His fingers lowered and intertwined with mine, his strong hold sending goosebumps across my skin. I followed a step behind him as he led me away from his family toward a nearby field. It only took a second for my eye to catch the beautiful black stallion in the distance. He was galloping through the tall, brown grass, as if burning off some steam before slowing to a stop, facing us head on.

My breath caught as I stared back at the horse. "Is that...?" I took a few more steps forward, breaking our connected hands. "Oh my gosh," I gasped, stepping up to the fence line. The horse took a few timid steps toward me, before picking up his pace, his head nodding up and down as he trotted right to me. I reached out my hand as he neared, brushing his nuzzle. "He's...I can't believe it."

"Glad to know I can still render you speechless." I caught the smug smile on his face from the corner of my eye as he stepped up beside me.

"Don't flatter yourself." I glanced at him. "The horse did. Not you." I continued to rub down his wiry coat. He was perfectly content allowing me to.

"What do you think?"

"He's beautiful. I'm amazed at how far he's come. I can't believe he's tamed. It's like he's a different horse."

"Glad you like him. Because he's yours."

"What are you talking about?" I spun to face him, my chest tightening.

"I bought him. I want you to have him."

"Wes, you know I can't accept him."

"You can. And I hope you can accept my apology for being a dumbass."

"Is that what this is? What he is?" I waved a hand toward the horse. "An apology?"

He shook his head. "They're two separate things. I want you to have him even if you don't accept my apology. I'm just hoping you'll accept us both."

I stared into his eyes as I mulled it over, knowing I couldn't go back to the way things were. "Hypothetically speaking, say I did. Where does that leave us?"

"Hopefully, naked in my bed." He winked with a smug grin.

"Wes," I chided, looking back at the horse.

"I'm kidding, Doc. Mostly." He cupped my cheek as he forced me to meet his eyes again. "I want to give us a real shot. I figure if this guy can change for the better, maybe there's hope for me."

"A real shot?"

"Yes. A couple. Girlfriend, boyfriend. Whatever label you want to put on us, I'll take. I just want you at the beginning and end of every day."

"I want that, too... But what happens when you get scared and act like an idiot again?"

"I don't know. You planning on breaking my heart, Doc?"

I linked my hands at the base of his neck. "You gotta trust

that I won't. Someone once told me trust is a beautiful thing when it's with the right person."

"Sounds like a smart guy."

"He can be. But it's rare."

"Ha-ha. Real cute, Doc." He gently pinched my side before moving in, his lips hovering near mine. "Is that a yes?"

"Yes," I breathed, lifting to my toes to seal the deal.

———

Two months later...

"Doc?" The sound of his voice alone lit me up inside, causing my thighs to clench together.

"In here," I hollered from my bathroom. I checked my appearance one more time, fluffing my hair before stepping out into the hallway.

Wes halted, his eyes doing an intense inspection of my small frame, which was barely covered by a thin, white tank and panties.

"How was your day, slick?" I reached above my head, planting my hand on the wall as I leaned into it, causing the tank to lift slightly and reveal a sliver of my stomach.

"Shit. But I have a feeling it's about to get a whole lot better."

I crooked a finger, imploring him forward.

He grinned, yanking the dirty cap he always wore for work from his head, and tossing it across the room. Reaching behind him, pulling his shirt from his body, he discarded it in the same hurried fashion as his hat. My body continued to heat up as I watched him prowl toward me.

"You got something in mind, brown eyes?"

"Besides wild, unadulterated sex?" I half-shrugged, keeping my voice nonchalant. "Not really."

His eyes lit with boyish mischief. "If I knew being in a relationship could be this much fun, I would've done it years ago."

"I make it fun."

He gripped the hem of my tank, pulling it up and over my head, exposing my bare chest. "That you do, Doc." He smiled down at my boobs, taking one in his large, calloused hand, and squeezing.

I clasped my fingers at the back of his neck, arching into him as his mouth wrapped around my nipple. His other hand dipped into my panties, finding me ready for him. I was always ready for him. In hindsight, I think I'd always been waiting for him to come along and set me free of my own self-doubt. Unlike Noah, Wes lifted me up instead of holding me down.

His kiss was full of color, his fingers full of magic as he stripped me and paved his way down to my center with his lips. My back pressed against the wall, my nails scraped into the paint as I struggled to ground myself. I was seconds away from flying toward ecstasy when his mouth was gone, forcing a whimper from my lips.

"Not yet, babe." Wes stood from his knees, toeing off his boots and dropping his jeans. "I wanna feel you around me when you come."

"Hurry," I demanded, glad we no longer bothered with condoms. I didn't think I had the patience now for him to roll one on.

Within seconds, he was inside me, my legs twisted around his lean waist in a vise grip. He kissed along my skin as he took me against the wall, the delicious burn of his five o'clock shadow coloring it pink. The air around us filled with the harmony of our moans and grunts and the smell of unfiltered sex.

"Fuck, Doc," he growled with another thrust. "I love you," he rasped into my neck.

I bit down on my lip before pulling his mouth to mine. Taking what was mine. It wasn't the first time he'd told me those three words. He made sure to say them every day, multiple times a day. But every time I heard them, my heart swelled a little more.

With a final thrust he tipped us both over the edge, filling me up inside. I flung my head back against the wall with a thud as I focused on my breathing. He held me close, the thin sheen of sweat coating our bodies causing me to slip a little. I laughed as he heaved me upward again, refusing to let go.

"You can put me down now."

"I'm not ready. I like being inside you."

I wiggled in his arms with a laugh. "I need to pee."

He kissed my lips, then slowly pulled out, setting me back down on my feet.

I slumped against the wall, still trying to recover. He reached for his jeans, tugging them on one leg at a time, then picked up my shirt to hand it to me. As I reached for it, his eyes went wide.

"What?" I asked, the look of panic on his face scaring me.

"Don't. Move." He dropped my shirt, blindly searching for his boot with his eyes pinned on the wall.

"Why?"

"The scorpion. It's by your head."

"Ha-ha. Real funny, slick. I'm not falling for that again." I put my hands on my hips.

"I'm serious, babe. Stay still." He lifted his boot up, rearing it backward.

My heartrate picked up when I realized he wasn't cracking a smile, or even a wink.

"Wes?"

He ignored me, his eyes focused just over my head and to the left a little.

When his boot suddenly flew toward me, I screamed, folding into a ball and covering my face. It all happened so fast—my scream, the loud smack on the wall, and the yell and groan from Wes as he crumpled forward from the contact of my knee to his crotch.

He fell into a heap on the floor, holding himself as he moaned. I dropped to my knees, feeling terrible.

"Damn, Doc." He pushed out a painful breath. "If you keep kneeing me in the balls, we may have zero chance of ever having kids."

My face blanked with his words, the remorse I was feeling suddenly overpowered by shock. "What did you just say?"

He rolled to his back, staring at the ceiling with a few louder breaths as I gently straddled his hips.

"You want to have kids with me?"

"If I didn't feel the way I do about you all the time, I'd think you sitting on me naked right now, asking me this, was a trap."

"Wes." I swatted at his chest.

Chuckling, he snatched my wrist, pulling me against him, giving me a tender kiss. "Yeah, babe. I want kids with you. I want it all: the kids, the dog, the house. I want every day for the rest of my life to be spent with you."

He rolled us on the floor, so his body blanketed mine. Brushing the stray hairs from my face, he kissed each of my cheeks and then my lips. Pulling back slightly, he peered down at me.

"This isn't exactly how I planned it. But if I always stuck to my plan, I wouldn't be here with you now. I love you, Devin. So damn much. But I don't want to go around town calling you my girlfriend anymore... I want to call you my wife."

My cheeks puffed with the breath I was holding as I felt the tears build in my eyes.

"What do you say, Doc? Will you marry me?"

I nodded my head, happy tears starting to spill over and stream down my face.

"I need to hear you say it, babe. These tears are confusing me." He swiped a few away with the pad of his thumb.

"Yes," I choked out, taking a deep breath, still nodding like a bobblehead. "Yes. A million times, yes."

EPILOGUE
WES

Six months later...

"Not having cold feet, are you?"

I lifted from where I'd been leaning against the old barn waiting for the wedding to start. I watched as Jenna strolled toward me in her bridesmaid gown. I'd always think she was beautiful, but in my eyes, she'd never hold a candle to Devin. Not that I'd ever say that out loud. I was doing my best to keep my dumbass comments to myself these days. "Nope."

No chance in hell would I be running from this wedding. At least, not without the woman I loved running along beside me. I'd snuck out here to let go of the past and thank God for giving me Devin.

She took the flask from my hand, the one I hadn't bothered to take a single sip from. "Good. Because I'd kick your ass if you broke my cousin's heart."

"You ain't gotta worry about that, Cricket. I know I'm lucky she chose to stick it out with me."

She gave me a fond smile before taking a small swig. She handed it back and I twisted the cap on, slipping it back into my jacket. "She's lucky, too, you know. It's time you realize that. Devin wouldn't stick it out if you weren't the best man for her."

As good as it felt to hear her say that, I still wasn't sure she was right. But I'd spend every day trying to prove her right. Trying to prove to Devin I was the man she deserved. I'd give her anything she ever wanted, starting with this wedding. It'd been her idea to keep it small and on our family farm. She didn't want a big fuss. Simple, laid back was how she'd described her dream wedding. The only thing she was adamant on was a magnolia bouquet.

"I don't want to just be the best man, Cricket." I puffed out my chest, straightening my lapels. "I want to be *the* man."

She chuckled, looping her arm through mine. "Come on, big guy. It's time for you to become *the man*, then."

———

FUMBLING WITH THE KEYCARD, I pressed my wife to the door of our hotel suite with my hips as I kissed down her throat.

My wife.

Damn. I never thought that'd feel so good to say.

Reaching behind her back, she snatched the card from

me, slipping it into the slot, twisting the knob open with ease, and all without looking. We stumbled into the room, never breaking contact.

"We're gonna talk someday about how you're so good at that," I mouthed into her throat before sucking hard on it. I planned to mark every inch of her, making sure every man she crossed paths with knew she was off the market.

"I have skills, baby. Ones you don't even know about."

I backed her to the bed, ready to take her fast and hard. We'd do slow and sweet later, because there was no way either of us had patience for that right now.

Proving my point, she spun us, putting me between her and the bed.

Maybe it was the alcohol. Maybe it was the fact that we were finally husband and wife. But I'd never seen this woman so dominant and needy. It was sexy as hell.

I stared down at her beautiful brown eyes as she slowly lowered to her knees in her wedding gown in front of me. The tip of her tongue darted out, licking those hot, pouty lips as she stared up at me under thick lashes. In that moment, I was certain of one thing: she drove me wild and my love for her would never be tamed.

"Drop your pants, slick. I'm about to rock your fucking world."

Ho-ly. Shit.

THE END

WANT to learn about everyone's favorite Dudley's bartender? Click here for Tempting Tim!

ENJOY THIS BOOK?

THANK YOU FOR READING!

I sincerely hope you enjoyed reading this book as much as I enjoyed writing it. If you did, I would greatly appreciate a short review on your favorite retailer, GoodReads, or Bookbub website. Or even all of the above! Just copy and paste!

Reviews encourage other readers to try out a book. They are critically important to getting the word out about a novel and mean the world to all authors.

I'd truly appreciate your help in sharing this book with the world. If you do, be sure to email me your review at melissa@melissaellenwrites.com, so I can thank you personally! Thank you again! You're the best!

NEVER MISS A THING
JOIN THE TEAM!

Join my VIP reader list and never miss a thing! Stay up to date on what I'm working on, my new releases, sales, and exclusive giveaways and sneak peeks by joining the VIP reader list HERE.

Are you a reader who likes reviewing?
If you like reading and reviewing, I'd love to have you on my ARC team! For more details CLICK HERE.

Blogger or Bookstagrammer?
If you'd like to be on my master blogger list, you can SIGN-UP HERE.

ALSO AVAILABLE FROM MELISSA ELLEN

BLACKWOOD SERIES

Billionaires and Rock Stars

A REASON TO STAY

THE ONLY ONE

A REASON TO LEAVE

FOREVER YOURS

BILLINGSLEY SERIES

Small Town Second Chance

REDEEMING LOTTIE

CHASING HANNAH

TAMING WES

TEMPTING TIM

MADE SERIES

Romantic Suspense

HONOR

BURDEN (Coming Soon)

SALVATION (Coming Soonish)

PREVIEW OF TEMPTING TIM

PROLOGUE - TIM

Sixteen Years Earlier...

"Nervous?"

"Nope."

I dropped my eyes to her knee that was bouncing so fast it reminded me of Thumper from Bambi. The tips of her fingers were planted deep above it. I was positive they'd leave an indention in her sun-kissed skin.

"Don't worry. It won't hurt," I reciprocated her lie, lifting my gaze to look straight ahead again as we continued to wait on the hard, wooden bench. Allowing them to linger on her for too long or travel up her bare legs the way they wanted to would be a mistake.

"I'm not scared."

I twisted my head to peer at her profile this time. Anxious tension was written all over her face. It made me want to slip my arm around her, pull her against me, and press a firm kiss on top of her head in hopes to lessen her nerves. But I wouldn't. That wasn't Conley's and my relationship.

The lying to hide our true feelings and thoughts, that was us. It's the way we'd always been and always would be. Ever since that scorching summer day she walked into my garage during one of my band's practices. It'd been three years. I could still remember it like it was yesterday, the vision of her as strong and vivid as the regret I still felt.

She'd been wearing a too-big-for-her vintage Led Zeppelin T-shirt tied in a knot at her waist and cut-off jean shorts that showed off her long, lean legs. Her curly, raven-colored hair had been piled high on her head with strands falling around her heart-shaped face, the same way it was today.

"He should be here," she said under her breath, glancing at the cell phone clutched in her other hand. I'd barely heard her over the loud music and the constant buzzing sound filling any potential silence.

"He will be." I had no idea if he would. If he didn't make it here soon, I'd kick his ass myself. Not that I minded being the fill-in. I'd do almost anything for Conley Logan. "Show me your sketch again," I added when my assurance hadn't seemed to soothe her.

For the first time since we arrived, a slight smile crept onto her lips. The tension eased from her small frame as she slipped her hand into the rear pocket of her jean shorts, pulling out a folded piece of paper with the sketch she'd drawn. She handed it to me. I unfolded the letter-sized sheet to stare at the black linework that filled the page. It was a collage of four delicate flowers, interweaved with small vines of leaves. Each one represented something significant to her, and they were woven together into a beautiful design.

"It's gonna make an awesome tattoo, Con."

She leaned into my side to look at it with me. The action was innocent, but still set off a heated, tingling sensation across my skin. "My parents are gonna flip when they see it. They'll probably kick me out of the house." She sat back with a huff, crossing her arms.

The immediate emptiness I felt at the loss of her touch mocked me. "If they do, you can always sleep in our basement."

"Jeez. Thanks. A cold, damp room with a couch that reeks of cat urine." She shoved at my shoulder lightly, another smile escaping. "I wouldn't want to put you out or anything."

I grinned at her, glad to see her nerves were momentarily forgotten. "Hey," I said with mock outrage, "Mr. Pickles is old. He can't help it if he has bladder-control issues."

"It's probably from all the pickle juice you guys give him. That can't be good for cats," she said through a chuckle.

"He likes it," I said with a shrug. It's how he got his name.

"Conley?" a deep voice interrupted her laughter. We both glanced up at a sizeable man covered in tattoos and piercings. A red, overgrown beard outlined his jaw, revealing only his eyes that were locked on Conley. "You ready?"

She turned her gaze back to me and then to the entrance, the light-hearted fun in her eyes gone again. "He's not here."

I hated the disappointment on her face, hated knowing

that I wasn't the one she wanted. I held back the rage at Bobby rushing through me, fighting to lash out. It was bad enough he'd been the one she chose. It only made it worse that he was never here when she needed him.

She'd been talking about her plan to get this tattoo on her eighteenth birthday for months now. He'd forgotten not only her birthday, but also that she wanted him by her side for this moment. Not that I needed the evidence, but it proved he was a self-centered moron.

"You'll be fine," I tried to assure her for the hundredth time. "It'll be over before you know it. The first one is always the scariest. After that, you'll be itching for another one."

Biting down lightly on her bottom lip, she nodded and stood as she ran her palms down her legs.

I stood with her, handing her the paper. "Don't forget this."

"Thanks." Our fingers brushed as she reached for it.

I drew back my hand before the instinct to hold hers took over. She turned, following slowly behind the man who'd be inking her skin. Watching her walk away, I took a step backward, lowering onto the bench again, when she spun to face me.

"I want you," she blurted, her eyes slamming shut as her cheeks changed to a light shade of pink.

I halted mid-sit and rose upright. The rapid thumping in my chest nearly drowned out her next words. "I mean, I need someone with me." She opened her eyes, meeting mine. "To distract me... Would you mind keeping me company?"

Before I could form any response, the door to the tattoo shop flew open, drawing both of our attention.

"You made it," she breathed, her words no longer directed at me, but at the guy walking through the door. The relief in her voice was another sharp stab to my chest.

"Hey, babe," Bobby greeted her, giving me a pat on the shoulder as he brushed by me headed for Conley. She wrapped her arms around him, burying her face in his neck. "You didn't think I'd miss this, did you?"

I bit down the sarcastic laugh wanting to burst from my mouth. We both knew this wasn't his priority or he wouldn't have texted me earlier today, asking me to bring her here. He'd completely forgotten until she messaged him to find out what time he was picking her up.

He'd bailed on her to go with one of our bandmates to check out a new guitar on sale in the next town over. He hadn't even told her I would be the one to pick her up. Her surprised expression when I showed up at her house told me that much. Doing what I did best, I lied to her, telling her he'd be meeting us. Then I fired off a text to him, demanding he get his ass here.

She drew back slightly, rising up on the balls of her feet to kiss him. His hands dropped to her ass and squeezed. Having already hit my limit of watching them together, I cleared my throat. "I'm just gonna..." I jabbed a thumb at the exit behind me. Neither one of them seemed to hear me nor remembered I was a few feet away. With a shake of my head, I turned on my heels and walked toward the door, shoving it open.

"Tim! Wait!" Conley hollered. Before I realized what was happening, her arms were wrapped around my waist and every inch of her body molded to mine with her cheek pressed to my chest. "Thank you," she whispered.

My heart stampeded in my rib cage once again as I willed my dick to behave and not react to her being flush against me. "No problem." The strangled words came out more as a deep croak.

She pulled from our embrace, lifting to her toes to plant a kiss on my cheek before she scurried off and back to her boyfriend's side.

"Yeah, thanks, man," Bobby said, his eyes locked on me as he lifted his chin and intertwined his fingers with hers. His appreciation was laced with a warning I didn't need.

I clenched and unclenched my fists, grinding my back molars, and shoved through the door again before the tension between Bobby and me turned into something more. It was the last thing our band needed—a fight over a girl who had never been mine.

I had nobody to blame but myself. He'd made a move when I hadn't. If I could go back to that day, three years ago in my garage, I would've grown a pair and staked my claim. She'd been there to see me, but somehow, she'd ended up with him. And now, there would never be an us.

WANT to learn more about Billingsley's favorite bartender? Click here for Tempting Tim!

ABOUT THE AUTHOR

Learn more about Melissa Ellen by visiting her website and subscribing for monthly updates in her newsletter!

Website:
www.melissaellenwrites.com

Contact me through any of the ways below:
Email me:
melissa@melissaellenwrites.com

Come Hang Out With Me!
Follow Me on Bookbub
Find Me on Facebook
Stalk me on Instagram
Join my Reader Group on Facebook
Become a VIP Reader

ACKNOWLEDGMENTS

I'd like to start by thanking all my readers! Thank you for spending your precious spare time picking up and reading my books. Thank you for your kind words.

Out of all the books I've written thus far, this one had to be the one I was most nervous about. Many of you fell in love with Wes over the last few books, so I didn't want to disappoint any of you. I truly hope you all enjoyed it and loved Wes and Devin as much as I did. This story was for all of you!

Thank you to all my lady friends over the years who helped inspire some scenes with our girls' night shenanigans. Christy, Kirstie, and Zima, that one fateful night was filled with so many laughs and good memories.

Samantha and Christy, you two are the bomb. You help make these books into greatness. Writing can be lonely, but having you two by my side, reading, and giving feedback as I go makes it so much more fun.

Thank you, Taryn. Girl, you are a blessing and I love, love working with you. I love all your little side comments in the manuscript as you read and edit. It really makes my day and you teach me something new in every book. Thanks for being there to polish my words and make them shine.

A special thanks to all the bloggers that have supported me. Especially, those who've been with me from the start—Mary, Katyln, Shelli, Teri, Jennifer, Lindsey and so many more I know I'm forgetting (sorry). You ladies are always the first to jump on my newest releases and spread the word. I can't thank you enough for your support. Also, thank you to my ARC team members. There are too many of you to list, but I want you to know I appreciate all that you do!

Last but never least, thank you to my family and friends. I love you more than you will ever know or I'll ever be able to show.

www.ingramcontent.com/pod-product-compliance
Lightning Source LLC
Chambersburg PA
CBHW071130200626
46817CB00018B/2525